CANDLELIGHT REGENCY SPECIAL

CANDLELIGHT ROMANCES

THE
CHEVALIER'S
LADY

Betty Hale Hyatt

A CANDLELIGHT REGENCY SPECIAL

Published by
Dell Publishing Co., Inc.
1 Dag Hammarskjold Plaza
New York, New York 10017

Dell ® TM 681510, Dell Publishing Co., Inc.

ISBN: 0-440-11015-7

Printed in the United States of America

First printing—January 1979

THE
CHEVALIER'S
LADY

1

The week preceding the ball at Columb Manor, I discovered the gold locket with the likeness of Jean de Rouvroy inside it, although at the time I could not know his name or where he came from. Indeed I knew nothing about him, so when I untangled the locket from a bush I was pruning, I was curious and held it up to the late September sun.

It was round in shape and bore an unusual crest, studded with what could only be rubies which formed a wheel containing a large emerald in the center and diamond-studded spokes emerging from it. The locket was attached to a slender gold link chain, with a clasp of another precious emerald.

At my touch, the locket sprung open, and the likeness of the young man stared back at me with wide dark eyes. Clearly he was aristocratic, with that high-bridged nose and finely cut features. In the other half of the locket was the picture of a young woman a few years older, I judged, but I was certain they were related, because of the similar look in the eyes and around the mouth. The picture of the woman loosened from the tiny gold prongs and fell out, along with a small folded piece of yellowed paper, and I caught it and unfolded it carefully. The words written in French were faded also, but the message was there for me to read:

"*Si je ne me trompes pas, je ne doutes pas que vous vendriez. Danielle.*"

"Unless I am mistaken, I do not doubt that you will come, Danielle."

It was as if I had intruded upon a secret that had been tucked out of sight for a lover to find in time for a rendezvous, and as I started to replace it with the guiltiness of one who has invaded that privacy, I noticed the finely wrought words inscribed inside the back of the locket: MARQUIS DU CHATEAU DE ROUVROY.

How odd, I thought, to find such a family treasure as this surely was; I believed it had belonged to one of those tragic families of the old Bourbon France.

It was nine years since the Reign of Terror, those days of the guillotine where thousands of French noblemen and women lost their heads; there had been floods of refugees fleeing to safety in England, exiling themselves from the old way of life as their kinsmen were dying, and eking out precarious lives by any means they could.

I stared at the faces of those two people inside the locket and wondered if they had escaped the guillotine and were now living in some dreary corner of London, putting up a facade that their highborn state had so ill prepared them for. Somehow I thought this highly unlikely as I studied the young man's noble features, for there was something arrogant and rebellious in those eyes and around the stubborn mouth that would prevent him from such a fate.

As I replaced the note and covered it with the picture, using my fingernail to secure it firmly within the gold tongs, I wondered if that rendezvous had been kept. Was the woman in this picture Danielle? I looked at the young man again; was he the Marquis de Rouvroy? Surely it was an empty title in this year of 1802, and in Napoléon Bonaparte's France?

But all this did not explain why such a locket was here at Columb Manor, a house on the Cornish coast so far away from either London or France. Impulsively I slipped it into the pocket of the burgundy merino gown I was wearing, wondering if Neville might have purchased the locket from a member of the family in need of money. Such occurrences were fairly common these days, but I was not at all sure of why Neville would buy such an extravagant piece of jewelry . . . and then not mention losing it. But why else would it appear in the shrubbery?

In an attempt to take my mind off these confusing questions, I returned to my rooms in the west wing of the house. I was excited about the ball planned for next week, but more excited about Neville's homecoming from London this day. He'd been gone a month, and that had seemed a long time; I knew too, that he was as anxious for the ball to turn out well as I was, for it was to be in honor of my betrothal announcement to Mr. Cameron Pennland of Penn Hall.

A nagging fear mingled with an unexplained reluctance claimed me in that moment; I had accepted Cameron's offer of marriage because I knew it would please my brother, just as it had pleased Cameron's aged father, Sir Avis, and Cameron's sister, Marietta.

"Now, we can be true sisters," Marietta had laughed, kissing me and practically saying "I told you so" with her eyes when Cameron had told our families. I knew her well enough to know she had wished this above all else, except for her own secret longings to "catch" my brother, as she had termed it.

She'd found him unbearably exciting in his aloof, secretive aloneness. "He is a man who has known deep sadness, Tamar," she'd informed me when we'd first become acquainted. "He is a man of mystery, and I find that most appealing; I adore older men with mysterious smiles behind their words and deep not-so-silent eyes. Neville Columb is that kind of man!" I had resented it at once, for Marietta was my own age, and I discovered I was a little too possessive about my brother.

Although Columb Manor was both Neville's and my own birthplace, I had not lived here since I was a baby. In the year after my birth, my father went to fight with General Wolfe in the American colonies and had died in the American War for Independence the following year. My mother, distraught and lonely, took me to London and succumbed to typhoid within that same year, and I was left in the care of a twenty-year-old brother who was finishing Oxford.

He in turn placed me in the care of my godmother, and for some eight or nine years I had a succession of nursemaids and governesses until my dear godmother died of the disease which took my mother. I was eleven when Neville sent me to Miss Rochelle's fashionable school for young ladies, and I remained there for seven years, at the end of which Neville unexpectedly came for me and took me away with him.

In those intervening two years we'd stayed in the stately house in St. James's Square. I kept house for Neville and gladly so; his job with the War Department now kept him in London, and those anxious years when he'd been abroad had receded into the past. Then our father's will was read belatedly, and to our relief Columb Manor was ours. Neville moved us gladly to Cornwall.

It was more than either of us had expected. A charming old house built in the late sixteenth century, it perfectly satisfied my own secret longing for a home, and I suspected it had affected Neville in the same manner.

We were fortunate that Penn Hall was our nearest neighbor, as Neville tried to point out often enough. Marietta was company for me, and Neville had known Cameron for years, he'd said, although Cameron was several years younger. "We knew each other in Paris at one time, our jobs with the War Department taking us there," Neville had explained.

Those years which had kept Neville out of England had been anxious ones for me, and now that they were over it meant he was relatively safe from the danger I'd always sensed surrounding his job. I'd known that he was an agent of sorts working in France during the Reign of Terror and in its aftermath, but of course I hadn't known exactly what it all entailed, nor had he spoken of it after he'd returned to take me from school.

Marietta Pennland believed she was the go-between of what she called the "romance of the year" between her brother and myself; but little did she know there was very little romance, on my part anyway. Cameron was good-looking, and he wanted a wife. Our houses were constantly open to each other, but it was only in the last two months that I'd really come to consider Cameron as my future husband. Even now I felt guilty about my reason for accepting his proposal.

I knew I was to receive a small inheritance from my parents upon my marriage. Neville had supported me most of my life, even at my godmother's, and later at the expensive school. I had never thought much about where his money came from, and it was only in those past three years that I knew we did not have much, or that Neville had very little income from our father's estate.

Thus when Neville took a keen interest in the old glassworks our ancestors had started at Columb Manor, and which had long ago been abandoned, I had seen something inside him and I knew that it would take a small fortune for him to start it going. My reason for accepting Cameron's offer of marriage was to present my own inheritance to my brother.

He'd been quiet that night when we were alone, after I'd told him. He'd not refused it, but had looked at me in a way that made my heart turn over in my adoration of him. "We shall go into partnership then, in the old glassworks, Tamar. I'm going up to London to talk with a man who's interested in small works like ours, and then I'll come back and we'll discuss it all properly after the ball. I insist we have it here, instead of Penn Hall." He'd smiled and then had looked into the dying embers of the fire on the hearth in our library, and placed aside his glass of brandy.

I could say nothing, so moved was I by my own emotions, which were so mixed at that time. But after a moment he said, "I'm glad you accepted Cam's offer, Tamar. It's a relief to know you'll be secure in such a family as the Pennlands of Penn Hall. You are happy, aren't you? It's what you want, isn't it?" He was searching my face with probing keenness, and I tried to hide my true feelings.

"I . . . I suppose so, Neville," but my voice had a breathless catch in it. "A girl simply doesn't get an offer like this every day, and well—" I swallowed hard, knowing a sense of devastation I never knew existed, and met the gray eyes, hoping he would understand. The incredible thing of it was that Neville did understand, at least in part, for he reached over and covered my hand with his own brown one.

"I know. It is just that you believed in love at first sight, and it didn't happen that way, did it? But good marriages are sometimes based on utter trust and in being friends first—a compatible relationship outrides everything else in the end. Love will come. In your first child, perhaps. Don't look so sad, my dear. I promise you, it won't be a bad thing. It will be good, because you will make it good."

Thus I had brushed aside my foolish and girlish ideals of magical romance, and saw it for all the truth that Neville had pointed it out to be. Yet I couldn't help thinking that he could not have known what was in my heart unless he had experienced something like it himself. I had gazed at him with new respect, and knew that Marietta had touched upon a truth about my brother that I had always felt too.

Now I washed the dirt from my hands, and heard the clatter of horses' hooves in the courtyard; my heart dipped in that excitement as it always did whenever I knew Neville was arriving, and I hurried down the stairs and outside to greet him.

He stepped down from his great handsome gray, Nester, and handed the reins to Simon. Neville was a good-looking man at thirty-nine, and I often wondered why some beautiful woman had not yet married him. His dark hair so like mine was thick and whipped now by the wind, unruly, with no touch of gray. The excellently tailored cut of the dark brown jacket fit his broad shoulders to perfection, the dark buckskin riding breeches tucked into mud-splattered Hessian boots encased well-muscled thighs.

I ran to him and he grabbed me and lifted me off my feet with one swing, then set me down and threw the saddlebag over his shoulder.

"My dear Tamar. What have you been doing this fortnight, except running wild like the gypsy you've become?" He brought his free arm around my shoulders and as I tried to keep up with his long stride across the courtyard into the house, I looked up into his eyes and saw the secret laughter in them.

"We've had a gale. You missed it," I said lightly, happy to see him. "And I suspect you've lots of gossip to tell me while we indulge in the lunch Melly has been preparing for you all morning. You must be famished! You've been riding hard since early morning? I'm right, aren't I?"

"How did you guess? You're getting wise to me, my dear girl. As far as that gale, it tore down into Tavistock last night and I was forced to put up at an inn on Dartmoor until it blew itself out. Otherwise I might have been here before now. And, yes, I'm famished. Ravenously so!"

We entered the house, and as we neared the stairs Neville stopped and took a large parcel from the saddlebag and sheepishly handed it to me.

"For you, miss," he said, kissing the top of my hair. "You deserve it, and more. In fact, more is on the way. Mind you, all these balls are opportunities to keep you looking less like a gypsy and more like a woman!" I laughed merrily as I took the splendidly wrapped parcel.

Reaching up to kiss his cheek, I undid the strings then and there, for he seemed to wish me to do so before him.

A sigh of pure joy escaped my throat as I lifted the beautiful gown from its wrappings. It was the

finest ivory muslin over French silk of deep amethyst. Beneath it lay a rich velvet cloak with a
hood and lining of cream-colored silk. I knew he
must have spent a fortune.

But the delight in his expression as he watched
me unwrap them was my equal reward, for I
could see he was taking great pleasure in giving
me these costly things. I knew all this at once as I
flung myself into his arms and hugged him, tears
wet on my cheeks.

"Oh, Neville!" I cried. "They're . . . just beautiful! How could you guess . . . How did you know
exactly what I wanted?"

He laughed. "When Melly told me you'd rum-
maged through the old chest and brought out our
mother's clothes, I thought it was time the
Columbs of Columb Manor presented a new face
to the Pennlands of Penn Hall! Now, off with you
and allow me to get the travel stains and mud
from my weary frame. Where's Rufus? I'll need
plenty of hot water if I'm to show my face at
Melly's table!" He kissed my forehead and said
gently, "I'll hurry back down. We've loads to talk
over."

It was that same evening that Neville spoke to
me of what was on his mind, and the old fears
came back to me, yet I was able to cast most of it
off because the preparations for the ball were
monopolizing both my thoughts and my energy.
After dinner we sat in the library, relaxed, sitting
across from each other. I was never more content
and wished it would go on forever like this.

Neville placed aside his brandy glass and said,

"I think you should know this, Tamar. The War Department may have use of me in the near future, and that is why I'm hoping you will have an early wedding. I want to see you settled and secure, and in a family like the Pennlands you will never be alone."

His words brought a chilling dread to my heart. "But why? I mean, we have a peace treaty with France, do we not? Why would the War Department need you?" He lifted a hand in a gesture that meant no explanation.

"It's an unstable situation, everyone knows that. But nothing has happened yet, and I have refused them for the moment in any case. Still, I'm relieved that the ball next week will betroth you to Cameron." He smiled, but I could not, for it seemed like a final preparation to rid himself of one last obstacle.

"Don't fret, Tamar. The good news is that I spoke to the man in London about the glass-blowing works, and he is very interested. He seems to know what he is talking about, and is willing to come down within a few weeks to look things over." His eyes held that special light that removed my anxiety in the moment.

"That blue-green glass our ancestors created is a real family secret, so it seems, and we must rediscover it. I'm excited about it, to tell the truth. It seems a worthwhile investment. I feel sure that the secret is somewhere under the silt of the years—those plans, I mean—and Rufus and I are going over tomorrow morning to give the place a thorough search. It will be interesting to learn how they made this unique blue-green shade of glass." He held up the goblet containing his brandy. He had discovered the pale blue-green crystal in the cellar three years ago, and even Melly and Rufus hadn't known they were there; but they both had been told by their families the story of the glass-blowing Columbs.

I was excited too. "It must have taken years for these first Columbs to have found the secret of this color, not to mention the very art of blowing them. But Marietta informed me that there was no little quarrel over the rights of that glass-house, in the beginning, between the Columbs and the Pennlands. And that was the reason for the abrupt abandoning of the works. She seemed interested, but Cameron was disinclined to comment on it either way."

Neville looked thoughtfully into the fire for a while, and absentmindedly took his pipe from his pocket and lit it. I sat back and watched him, feeling that nameless dread steal over me. I wanted my brother to be satisfied as well as prosperous in this new venture, and I knew that I would give all my inheritance to him without any qualms to see it through. There were times when I wished I didn't love him so much, and those were the times when I felt he would go out of my life and never return. I suppose that came from having no parents; I always feared abandonment.

After a while he stirred, and as the clock from the stables struck the quarter hour, he said, "I'm ready to call it a day, kitten. There's a big day ahead of us tomorrow, and the more rest you get tonight, the more beautiful you'll look in all your new finery for the lucky Cameron!" He laughed as

I playfully threw the small cushion at him, and he caught it. "By the way," he said, looking down at me as he stood up, "may I inquire where you got that necklace, my dear? I haven't seen it before, have I? It's most unusual."

He was speaking of the locket I'd found, and which I had inpulsively worn when I dressed for dinner. I hadn't been able to get it out of my mind, and I'd wanted to ask Neville about it, but had forgotten it in all the evening's activity.

I stared at him now, and then I laughed. "I had thought you might enlighten me, dear brother. I found it in the garden and somehow had the idea you might have purchased it somewhere in your travels, and then lost it."

He shook his head, but did not ask me to take it off. "I've not seen it before. No. Perhaps it belonged to our mother. She had a lot of things left here, you know, but I don't recognize it. Perhaps Melly can enlighten you. But I see no reason why you shouldn't keep it, do you? It's very attractive around your pretty neck."

It was on the tip of my tongue to tell him what I'd discovered inside, but Rufus entered then with the candles to light our way up the stairs, and Neville said, "Go on up, Tamar. I'll help lock up, and I want to talk with Rufus now. Good-night." He kissed my cheek, and took the candle from Rufus and placed it in my hands.

"Good-night, Neville." I believed I was a little uneasy as I made my way up to my rooms, wondering if this locket had indeed been my mother's. But something told me even then that it was not; intangible though it was, I felt I would come close to learning the truth of why it was here in Columb Manor.

All week preparations had been in progress for the ball; the old beams had been polished and smelled of beeswax and lemon oil, and Arlie had outdone himself with the flowers he'd brought in from his gardens. It was true that Columb Manor was not the showplace that Penn Hall was, but it didn't lessen the charm and beauty of the old house with its two small courtyards in the back.

The front of the house faced the sea, set back a little way, protected by groves of copper beeches and limes. A wide vista of lawn with a lovely walled-in garden to the southwest provided privacy from the winds that blew in from the Atlantic.

The old hall, quite small in comparison to Penn Hall's, was nevertheless a beautiful room in all its antiquity, with the minstrel's gallery at one end and where, on this night, tubs of perfumed flowers had been placed among the small tables set up with chairs for the guests to sup at later.

Melly had brought in extra help, and the tantalizing scents from her kitchens had drawn one and all there to sample a little treat of her pies and goodies.

On the day of the ball, Neville went out to the old glassworks, and after a full day of trying to help Melly, but more often getting into her way, I finally went to my rooms to prepare myself for the ball.

Effie was already there, filling the copper tub with hot water for my bath. She too was flushed with all the excitement of the evening's coming festivities.

"Oh, miss! Melly do say 'ee are to have a bite to eat, 'ee are, after 'ee bath an' all a'fore 'ee go down to the hall. Her'm say 'twill be a long spell till 'ee get a chance to eat, what with all them guests acomin' to excite 'ee. Lawks, but bain't 'ee excited? I'm to take a tray down to the library for 'ee and 'ee brother."

"All right, Effie," I said, looking around the room and seeing that she had already laid out the new gown for me. How beautiful it was; Neville must have paid a fortune for it, not to mention the other gowns that had come down from London during the week, and were, according to Neville, my trousseau. He had evaded the questioning gaze I'd given him, but had been extremely pleased when I'd tried on all the new gowns for him. So I'd said nothing.

But I called out, "Effie, has my brother returned from the glass-house?"

"Oh, yes, miss, that do be so, Mr. Neville be returned and shut up in his study with Rufus, and at his elbow, all excited like him'ud found a treasure an' all, I do say so, miss. But hap' 'ee'll know about them plans 'ee brother found only this morning?" She came in from the bath, carrying the cans with her, her eyes bright blue in her pink face.

I nodded, and she went on. "Well, Melly do say that the master found another set what matched them and he an' Rufus are thicker'n thieves down in his study, that's what this very minute. But 'ee bath be ready now, miss. Jackie do be acomin'

27

with more water for 'ee. There he be now, speak of angels." She hurried to the door to the timid knock. "Lawks, but 'ee came quicker'n I thought 'ee would, Jackie me pet! Put the tin down in there, and get on 'ee way. Master'll be awantin' him hot water too! Get on with 'ee!" But she grinned at the young boy who was Simon and Lena's son. Simon was Effie's brother, who worked in the stables; Lena was the dairy woman and she often helped Melly in the kitchens.

After he left, I said, "Have the musicians already come, Effie? I thought I heard a carriage drive up a short while back. I hope none of the guests have started to arrive as yet!" I hurried into the small room off my bedroom, and Effie, laying out my underthings, called in, "Aye, miss, thet what 'ee heard were the musicians, all right, they be! And what a ruckus they made, but Melly set them down at her table, any ruckus would stop, lor' if'n they wouldn't! And Dolly be there makin' eyes at young Will. They do be sweet on each other, her'n young Will." She giggled.

"Will? And who is young Will, Effie?" I asked, pouring bath oil in the water, the scent rising like the perfume of violets.

"Oh, miss, young Will, he be one of them musicians! Grooms, from down Helston way, he do. Him and Dolly, what be my cousin an' all, 'ee see, plan to be wed. We both be awearin' them new gowns what you gave us, miss. And Dolly be already in her pink'n, fussin' like somethin' 'ee never have seen afore, now if she don't!" Again she giggled, and I had to smile as I looked over my shoulder at her.

"And will you be wearing your new blue one, Effie? Will your beau be here too tonight?" I had given the two girls the gowns, and never had I experienced more enjoyment than I did watching them try them on that day; the pleasure they had derived from the gowns I myself had grown tired of, had been a treat in itself.

"Oh, yes, miss, I wouldn't miss wearin' me new gown for nothin', no I wouldn't! Robbie he be acomin' too. That be my boyfriend, miss. Robbie Stowe, what lives down in Barton Stowe, if 'ee might remember. But we bain't serious like Dolly and her young Will, no. Best wait, so Simon says, miss. But that don't keep us from courtin'."

"You're right, Effie, or so Simon is. Well, don't be late in dressing, now. I'll have my bath, so you can clean up around here, and be ready." I turned and closed the door.

I was glad to strip off my clothes and sink into the large tub. For better than an hour I soaked my body, cleaning my nails and washing my hair. When I stepped from my bath, I rubbed my skin with the nubby white towel until it glowed and stood before the long oval-shaped looking glass that was in the corner.

I inspected my body and my face. The moisture had made the tendrils of my hair curlier, and my eyes had a smoky color about them, wide eyes with short stubby lashes more like brushes dipped in soot, I thought; my mouth was a trifle too wide, with full pink lips. My smooth high cheekbones, so tanned, and my slightly slanted eyes gave my face an almost oriental look I'd been told on occasion.

I was quite tall, very slender, with high full breasts; my thighs and hips were shapely and my legs were long and slender like a young boy's; I knew I did justice to the beautiful gowns in fashion at the moment, and as I rubbed rose lotion into my skin, it was not Cameron I was thinking of, but of the young man in the locket, wondering where in this world he was at this moment.

Was he free as I was? Was his heart light and merry tonight? Or had some fate robbed him of the happiness he might have had?

Try as I might, I could not rid my thoughts of him, and I felt more than a little guilty, for I did not even know who he was. And why hadn't I been thinking of the man I had promised to marry?

My thoughts caused me to rub fiercely at my hair until it was dry, and I brushed the curls into place; it was a thick mane of long deep rich brown curls, glossy as rubbed mahogany. I took a certain pride in its abundance, for more than once I had been complimented on its beauty. I had not cut it, as was the fashion in London, and Neville had said of it, "Your hair is your beauty, Tamar. It's always a pleasure just to look upon it." And of course that had meant more to me than even Cameron's compliments, or Marietta's envy of its rich color.

I arranged the curls so that they touched my smooth, browned shoulder, and threaded a wide velvet ribbon through them.

The eyes in the glowing face that stared back at me from the mirror took on a strange light, enhanced by my own excitement as well as by the new gown I had hooked in place.

Neville had impeccable taste I thought at once as I ran a critical eye over the deep amethyst silk underneath the ivory muslin edged in gold. That he'd gone to Madame Rose, who had my measurements, had helped, but nonetheless, the gown was perfection, suiting my figure exquisitely.

I reached for the pearls that had belonged to my mother, and I found to my dismay that the clasp was broken; impulsively, I picked up the beautiful locket and looked at it, knowing it was a far more rare piece of jewelry. Neville had said I should keep it, hadn't he? I would wear it tonight then, I decided, and I felt a thrill of sorts as I slipped it around my neck, the jewels sparkling between my breasts in the low neckline of my gown.

I turned as Effie entered with the tray she was carrying to the library, and her eyes nearly bulged out of their sockets as she stared. "Lawks, miss! Now if 'ee don't be a sight for sore eyes! A real beaut', if 'ee don't mind me sayin'."

I laughed. "I don't mind your saying so, Effie, not at all. It is the nicest of compliments. Thank you." I noticed her eyes lingered on the locket and I somehow didn't care to explain where it had come from, so I said, "Effie, I'm going down to the library now, so I'll just take the tray down myself with me. My brother should be there soon, and you must get on with your own toilette after you finish here."

"Aye, miss," she said, pleased, and opened the

door for me as I took the tray and stepped out into the corridor.

"Remember, you're to help serve in the Hall tonight, and let me know if there are any problems you can't take care of," I told her.

"Aye, miss. That I will, for sure now." And I left her.

There are rare moments in life when one has a sense of belonging for the first time; I suppose to have that happen and to be made aware of it, poignantly so, one must first have the experience of never having belonged to a house or home before, and as I walked through the corridor and went downstairs slowly into the hall below, I was aware of how that sense of belonging swept around me, enfolding me in its warmth so that I almost felt lightheaded with it.

I could not think how I should ever be able to leave this house after marrying into the Pennland family. In fact I could not bear the thought, so I closed my mind to it, accepting what I had here in this one lovely moment.

That the servants had taken such pride in this evening's festivities proved their devotion and loyalty, as did the way they had scrubbed and cleaned and polished the whole house until it shone like a rare jewel. The huge cartwheel of the chandelier hung from the lofty ceiling, its hundreds of candles to be lit in an hour by Rufus and Jackie. I couldn't resist the urge to peek into the great hall where the dancing would take place. The room was quiet now, in the shadows of dusk, yet the great fireplace at one end was aglow with fire to ward off the chill of September.

Pots of late summer roses and camellias scented the air, and ivy twined around the carved posts to give the room a festive air: the old gallery around the hall was set up for the supper tables, and on the raised dais the musicians had already arranged their instruments. I was pleased with all I saw, and suddenly had a strange tight feeling in my throat as I desperately wished time would be suspended, and I would live forever in this moment.

Then I shrugged and laughed at myself for being so silly. Everything and everyone moved toward the future, nothing could be caught and held a prisoner of time, I thought as I quickly crossed the foyer to the library and went inside.

Neville was not down yet, and I set the tray down on a gleaming tabletop and gazed around this room. It too would be open to our guests, and the wide French doors to the garden would be open, for Arlie and Rufus had festooned the walled-in garden with Chinese lanterns soon to be lit. Now the copperish pink of the sun, already down beyond the cliffs into the sea, left an opalescent veil to shimmer in the flower-scented garden, and I turned to the room.

It glowed in the firelight which was faintly reflected in the mullioned windows and which touched the rich Axminster carpet so that its colors stood out with more softly glowing blues and pinks. We used this room more than any other simply because it was designed so, being in the southwest corner. It was comfortable, and the furniture was arranged around the huge fireplace. Flowers cut fresh daily were always in this room, but tonight it seemed as if Arlie had gone wild with his color scheme; pots of deep purple and red fuchsia were placed about, bronze and gold chrysanthemums stood in corners and were reflected in the long gilt-framed mirror over the fireplace.

I turned as the door opened and Neville walked in and I hurried over to him. "Neville!" I couldn't keep the joy from bubbling up, "Isn't it all just— just heavenly beautiful tonight? The house—oh, I can hardly wait to see all the lights aglow in that chandelier, and to hear the music in the old hall. Don't you feel it too? This wonderful sense of belonging to Columb Manor?"

He had taken my hands in his, looking down at me with that way he had of making me feel special; how handsome he was this night, in the dark gray-blue velvet coat that fitted him to an elegance. "Lord of the Manor," I teased him.

"And you, Tamar Columb, have been magically transformed into the mistress of the Manor! What justice you do to that gown!" he admired, holding me at arms length. "And what's all this talk of *belonging*?" He lifted dark eyebrows and chuckled. "I was sure only I could feel that way about this old ramshackle house our family built and left to seed."

I laughed too, delighted. "Left to seed and now bursting forth into full bloom! Well, you might as well share the supper Melly made for us, and you can tell me all that you discovered out at the glass-house today."

"So you have heard? I wanted it as my little surprise." He watched as I brought the tray over and began to fill his plate with the hot Cornish meat pie only Melly could make so well, and then filled a goblet with a rich red wine from our cellar, passing it to him. "But I did unearth what I always knew would be there to coincide with those plans I found in the study. So when our man comes down from London, Columb Manor just might be in the glassblowing business again, as it was in the late sixteenth century when it started. It's going to be a challenge."

"And one you will welcome, I should think," I added as we raised our glasses to each other.

For one long moment he was silent. "All made possible by you, my dear Tamar. You will share it with me, for it will mean a family trade, and you are all I have. I'm counting on you to provide nephews and nieces, even if they are Pennlands." It hurt my heart, but I agreed, and wished I could remain a Columb forever.

"I could never quite understand just why you weren't matched up in a marriage long ago by some fascinating woman and had your own brood of children, Neville." I tried to sound light. "Hadn't you ever thought of marrying and having a family, instead of having to look after a sister?" It had occurred to me more than once that I had probably been his reason for remaining a bachelor, and that to see me married would give him a certain freedom even now. A pang like that of jealousy struck my heart.

He gazed at me with laughter in his eyes. "Now, I know you have grown up, my girl," he said in the old teasing manner. "Only a woman who has caught her victim will look at a comfortable old bachelor and ask that question, 'Why haven't *you* a wife, good sir?' Has it ever oc-

curred to you I might enjoy the mysterious role of
a free man who likes looking after a gypsy sister,
always eluding the matchmaking mamas constantly
on the lookout for my kind to wed their daughters?
Even our Miss Marietta, from all I can detect, has
scheming designs on this confirmed bachelor, am I
right?"

"Well, designs or not, you are an attractive
man, Neville dear. And while I own that Marietta
is a . . . flirt, she is an attractive one, you must admit. She certainly is spellbound by the aura of
mystery that surrounds you and your secret life."

He chuckled, somehow untouched by Marietta's
desires and said, "Marietta Pennland might as
well save her charms and energy for some other
lucky man, my dear. I fancy that she might switch
her affections very quickly when the right man
comes along."

I didn't add that Marietta had declared that
Neville *was* the right man for her, and that I'd
known she was hoping to open the ball with him
this night. The muted sound of the carriage
wheels on cobblestones in the courtyard told us
that our first guests were arriving, and Rufus hurried in to take our trays and to announce, "The
Pennlands have arrived, m'lord."

Rufus, wrinkled, brown as wood, with a heavy
shock of white hair that stood up stiffly, was
dressed quaintly in pale blue livery. His kneepants
were brushed to a sheen, and he wore white stock-
ings and black shoes with shiny silver buckles.

"Show them in, Rufus," Neville told him. "Our
evening is about to begin. Please bring in that
bottle of champagne, the one I picked out earlier.

We shall have to toast m'lady and her . . . happiness, shall we not?"

"Aye, m'lord, that we do, that we do."

Cameron Pennland was not as good looking as my brother, but he was considered to be quite a handsome man. Some six years younger than Neville, he had an air of congeniality which made him easy to like. His fair hair caught the yellow light from the candles when Rufus lit them, and although his skin was not as dark as Neville's, it was pleasantly ruddy in color, and his blue eyes sparkled as they rested on my face when he came in with Marietta and their father and aunt.

But it was Marietta who rushed over to me and greeted me warmly with her embrace. "Tamar Columb! You are positively glowing tonight! What a ravishing gown! Oh, but I know it was dear Neville who brought it down from London for you! He certainly has taste, and you're so lucky!" Her own blue eyes turned on Neville, and anyone with an ounce of intuition would see how she felt about my brother.

But I could not be angry with her, for I knew how right she was about him.

"Thank you, Marietta," I smiled, and found that I could admire her own lovely golden gown of silk organza, like a cloud of light. Her red-gold curls were caught up in a jeweled clasp, and I was sure no eye could resist resting on her lovely, almost petulant mouth and enticing dimples. "My brother is indeed responsible for my gown, and I am lucky that he does have such taste." I turned to greet Cameron.

His hand was warm and brown and he held mine possessively; his eyes told me that he approved of me. I had reason to believe, too, that he would be a possessive husband, and perhaps resent my affection for my brother.

"Tamar. My sister is right, for once. You are positively glowing. How . . . lucky for me." And he kissed my cheek, then kept my hand in his as I turned to greet old Sir Avis and his sister Clovis.

The old man was like a withered, aged lion, sitting in his chair the servants had brought in. His face was lined and he wore a long mane of hair tied back in the old-fashioned pigtail which had once been the same brilliant shade as his daughter's. I think he was pleased that his son had finally decided to wed, even though the match would not benefit him financially.

"My dear," he said in a strong, gruff voice, "you are making me happy this night, by betrothing yourself to this son of mine. It is time that I get some heirs, is it not, Clovis?" He took my hand from Cameron and held it for a long time, patting it.

Clovis, a soft woman who always seemed to be in a swathing of heliotrope grays, but who was so comfortable as to make everyone around her so, smiled and said fondly, "But Avis dear, you already have heirs, and that you must never forget. But, my dear Tamar, you are a vision of loveliness, and my nephew here stands to gain very much indeed when you are his wife. We are happy, and to think of you with us at Penn Hall is a happy thought." She kissed my cheeks warmly, smelling faintly of lavender.

"May I then suggest we toast to that?" Neville said, his eyebrows lifted as he gazed upon us all. I knew I was flushed from all the praise, and I was glad to help Rufus pass around the beautifully pale green-blue stemmed goblets.

"Penn Hall has nothing quite so remarkable as this splendid glass. What a shame our family did not take to the glassblowing art as the Columbs have!"

"We were not given to art, such as it was," said Sir Avis's sister, holding her glass up to the light. "But what treasures these must be to you, Neville dear. You must be proud of them. I should think these alone would be worth a fortune."

Cameron came to me then, and took my free hand in his and looked down into my face. "I have the treasure of Columb Manor, and it is time we toast to this, not its heirlooms." And as we lifted our glasses, we heard the sounds of arriving guests that told us our evening was about to begin.

Neville opened the ball by leading me out onto the floor, with Cameron and Marietta following to the tune of the Cornish "Furry Dance." Lights dazzled us as we danced the first measures, and then Neville handed me to Cameron, bowing to me, and the cotillion began.

We could not talk as easily as he wanted to talk while dancing the cotillion, but when our hands met, he said, "We cannot put off our wedding too long, Tamar. Father isn't all that well, and he would like to see us settled. Would you like to set a date this night? Perhaps a month from now?" He lifted his brows, the blue eyes eager and demanding, but my heart sank. "So soon?" I murmured, and dipped a curtsy, only to meet his eyes again and notice that he was staring intently at the locket at my breast. Then I was whirled away from him by another partner.

It was a beautiful ball. The candles burned with brilliance; jewels shone, satins and silks and rich velvets shimmered, and the faces of people I'd never known swam around me, a crowd composed mostly of the Pennland relations and friends, and very few of my friends and acquaintances.

Occasionally I glanced around the room and saw Effie and Dolly, dressed in their pretty gowns, strutting with trays of drinks or refreshments, and I knew they were having a grand time. Once I looked over and found Melly speaking to Neville, peeking through one of the doors. She too was dressed in her best gown with a snowy white muslin fichu around her ample shoulders, her face round and flushed and proud as a peacock enjoying what she and the rest of Columb Manor had made possible to happen.

I was content as I caught her glance, and we both smiled. I did not want this to end, and hated myself for thinking it could go on, for I knew Cameron had made it clear he wanted no delay in our wedding.

It was still early in the evening; Cameron was deep in conversation with the husband of one of his cousins from St. Ives, and Marietta was dancing with a handsome young man I did not know, but I knew they were flirting with each other when I glanced around to find Neville. As I could not see him, I went in search of him, and found Rufus looking for me instead.

"Oh, Rufus. It's near time for the break, and I cannot seem to locate my brother. Have you seen him?"

"Aye, m'lady. 'Hap he do send a message for 'ee, he do. Come to the study, he say, an' right away."

"Oh? Is something wrong, Rufus?" I frowned.

"Oh, I bain't think so, m'lady, no." He puckered his lips, and because he didn't seem the least perturbed, I said, "All right. I will go. And Rufus, it is going beautifully, isn't it?"

He arched thick, bushy brows, looking every inch a pixie. "Eh? Oh, aye, m'lady. 'Tis well. Very well, that do be so."

"Thank you, Rufus. Thank you and Melly and Arlie and everyone, for making it all so lovely. My brother and I—" I couldn't find the words.

The old man was startled, but prim and proper as he was, he bowed stiffly, and I saw the faint curve of a smile on that mouth. I turned and walked away toward the study.

The door to the study was closed; I didn't knock as I usually do, but just opened it and heard the voices speaking in rapid French.

The scene before me was one I will never forget; Neville was standing facing a man whose back was to me, a tall, lean man in a dark blue coat, the shapely head of black hair just curling at the edge of his coat collar. But it was Neville's face that shocked me. It was chalk white, his gray eyes flashing like steel.

"Nom de Dieu," he said in a low voice, his French as easily spoken as was his English, and be-

cause I knew my French well enough, I could follow what was being said. "Who the devil do you
think you are to come into my home like this?
What do you want of me?" He was angry, and for
one moment I thought he was going to strike the
man, but he did not. Suddenly the man turned to
face me, stepping aside from Neville.

"*S'il vous plaît,*" he said in a husky but pleasant
voice. "Please join us, Mademoiselle Columb. You
are the sister of Monsieur Columb, *n'est-ce pas?*"

Nothing had prepared me for this; there was no
mistake, I told myself as my pulse pounded
maddeningly and I met the dark, arrogant eyes of
this man. It was the face of the man in the locket,
older to be sure, and very brown, but the same
face. No youth here, but a man, arrogant and
cruel as his fine dark eyes ran over me searchingly,
and I could only stare at him in dumb astonishment, feeling a shiver of extreme excitement as
well as fear crawl up my spine.

Involuntarily my fingers closed over the locket
at my throat, and I felt my cheeks burning as if
I'd been caught in a naughty escapade.

"Leave her out of this," Neville said in a voice
that caused my skin to prickle with terror. "*Oui,*"
he said slowly, "she is my sister, and because we
have guests, monsieur, she must return to them.
Please go, Tamar. Leave us quietly." He was imploring me to understand that this was his affair
and he would take care of it.

"I think not, monsieur. Mademoiselle is one of
the reasons for which I came to Columb Manor."

I believe it was then I became aware of two
things, but they happened so quickly that I can

never be sure which happened first; something moved in one of the corners behind the heavy green velvet curtains just as Neville said, "What is it you are after, monsieur?"

The Frenchman's words stung like acid. "I will not forget Danielle, monsieur. You are the Englishman who robbed her and betrayed my parents. You are going to pay."

I saw a wiry man emerge from behind the curtains with a gun in each hand, but it was Neville's face that kept me from crying out in a warning; he stared at the man in front of him, pain in every line.

"Danielle! What the devil do you mean!?" And his eyes found me.

In that instant, a pair of strong hands dug into my arms, pinioning them back, and I saw the man from behind the curtain strike Neville's head. Just as I saw Neville's shocked expression, a sweet-smelling cloth was held over my face.

I struggled, the scream dying in my throat, but my struggles were all in vain as a blackness I never knew existed engulfed me, and I sank into the terror of its oblivion.

2

Strangely enough it was a rocking motion that awakened me. I opened my eyes to a streak of light streaming in through a crack in the drawn curtains. Slowly I became aware of the sound of water lapping gently somewhere nearby, and of the dark red of the unfamiliar curtains, and of how warm I was. Then I glanced down at the heavy garment flung over my body, and at once I saw that I was fully dressed in my ball gown, and that the red cloak spread over me was my own.

Memory flooded like a flash in my brain, and I sat up in shock. The room that met my eyes was one I had never seen before, and I realized that it was a ship's cabin. I tried to think clearly, and as if I had come a great distance across time, I remembered the ball at Columb Manor, the night, and like a nightmare returning to mar that bright memory, the scene in Neville's study rushed forward.

Neville!

My heart pounded wildly as I recalled his face and the gun that had struck his head. I'd been abducted by the Frenchman! I shuddered, remembering.

Not able to face these terrible truths, I looked around the room at the dark wood paneling, the soft carpet, the heavy table and chairs under the windows. I stared in awe at the beauty of this tiny cabin, the glass cabinet which held silver goblets and some leather-bound books, an inkwell, with quill. There was a round globe in the corner on a wooden frame, and a lantern hung directly over the table from low, polished beams.

My eyes found the small curtained-off alcove which revealed a washstand and an elaborate porcelain ewer and bowl, with a mirror attached to the wall above. There was a large copper can beside the washstand, and a thick white towel with soap on a three-legged stool. I gazed at everything, and then I stared at the bunk bed I had slept in, enclosed by heavy red velvet curtains.

I slipped from the bed, aware that my gown was crushed, and that my mouth felt as though wool had been stuffed inside it. My long hair had come unpinned. I moved across the room without making a sound, and looked cautiously out the window.

I saw that the ship was anchored in a bay; rocks the color of ripe plums rose up out of the sea against the golden sky that shimmered with the glow of the setting sun. Seagulls swooped joyously through the air around the rocks and the ship, plunging again and again into the water for food.

Wisps of lazy blue smoke curled upward from somewhere, and the tantalizing smell of roasting meat, freshly baked bread, and coffee caused me to realize just how famished I was, and that hunger took precedence over my fears.

I could not know where I was, or how long ago the drama in Neville's study took place, but if Neville were dead, what fate then awaited me? I brushed aside this thought, and tried not to fan the flames of those fears that tormented me.

The Frenchman, of course, was my enemy. My hand went to the locket still dangling around my neck, and I remembered that this must belong to him. I bit my lower lip to keep it from trembling, and I wondered what he might do to me if he saw it around my neck, or in my possession. Hurriedly I removed it and placed it in the pocket hidden within the folds of my skirt, blessing the dressmakers for designing such secret places!

Again I looked around the room, and down at my gown; its beautiful amethyst silk was wrinkled, the ivory muslin untidy, and I felt far too warm and sticky with heat. Impulsively I hurried over to that little alcove, pulled the curtain, and peered into the mirror. I was indeed a sorry sight, my hair unbound and a mass of tangled curls. I dipped my fingers into the water can and discovered it was quite warm. So, someone had been in here while I slept, and not too long ago.

Without another thought I stripped off my gown and underclothes, and washed my body from my face to my feet in that delicious water, using the soap, and drying with the towel. I shook my clothes and then redressed quickly and used

the comb I saw there to comb the tangles. Just
then the door swung open, and a tremor shook
me, for I did not know what to expect. But whatever was to happen, I would face it with defiance.

A strange little man appeared, and I had never
seen such a creature in my life. He resembled a
monkey, his wizened face curved up into a perpetual smile, the dark eyes sparkling black. He wore
a funny little three-cornered hat on his rather
large head, and baggy pants and a white shirt that
had seen much wear. He carried a large tray upon
which were several covered dishes, and when he
saw me, he broke out in a rash of foreign words I
couldn't understand. Judging by the look in his
eyes, he was as wary of me as I was of him, but his
smile never vanished. Too late I realized that I
was staring at him, and that he was frightened of
me for doing so. It was only then that I guessed
the truth; his mouth had actually been *carved* in
that shape.

He placed the tray down on the table, and
started to back out of the room, but the Frenchman appeared, pushing the little man back inside
the room with him. I stepped back, my heart racing madly, and I felt the blood rush to my face.

"Mademoiselle Columb. So you are awake?" I
remembered the husky pleasantness of his voice
with what amounted to shock, all of it rushing
back to me sharply, vividly. He wore no jacket
now; the white shirt was open at the front
showing brown skin and dark hair on the broad
chest, the sleeves rolled to the elbow revealing
strong bronzed arms. I was aware—and angry with

myself for being so—that he was by far the most handsome man I had ever seen.

Caught as I was, I didn't answer, standing almost guiltily in the alcove. But he was aware of my uncomfortableness, I knew, for the smile under the dark mustache told me so. He was amused at my expense, and I resented it at once. Odious man! I despised myself for blushing like any common maid.

"I see you have made use of the fresh water that Jock brought in for you, mademoiselle. He has looked after you since we left your shores last evening." He spoke in English but with a heavy French accent, and such aristocratic arrogance that I immediately felt disdain for the insufferable man!

When I didn't answer, he went on, "*S'il vous plaît*, Mademoiselle Columb. This is Jock, my cabin boy. He has brought food, which he himself prepared. Jock," he said as he turned to the little man whose eyes now were flashing from his master to me and back again with such adoration I could hardly believe it, "this is Mademoiselle Columb. *Enchanté, n'est-ce pas?* She is our guest, and we must make her welcome."

"*Oui*," said the little man, "*mais oui!*" And he bowed to me, laughing in a high-pitched laugh that had an eerie sound to it, and the Frenchman laughed heartily too. He motioned for Jock to go, and as he left, I looked to the Frenchman and our eyes met and held.

"You must not be frightened of Jock, mademoiselle," he said casually. "Jock is like a child, you see. He likes to win favors of those he instinctively knows he must serve."

I found my voice then. "What—what is wrong with his face?"

The man had the audacity to smile, but he answered my question. "He was carved like that many years ago. He is a dwarf, you see, and he is Moorish. The court he was sold into as a very young man bought him for that very smile—which had been carved to insure that people would laugh at him. His first owners knew how to do that, you see. It is an old but cruel custom. I found him starving to death, left behind after a pirate raid, and he has served me well since that day."

I stared at him in shocked silence.

"Will you join me in some dinner, mademoiselle? I fancy that you must be ravenous. You slept soundly, you know, all through the night's voyage, and I had not the heart to waken you, for you slept on through this full day!"

He waited, and when I did not move, he gestured to the table. "Jock would be hurt if we did not enjoy this food he prepared. Come, *s'il vous plaît*. It will do you good, and afterwards we can talk."

I knew he was aware of every detail of my appearance, especially of the low-cut gown which I now felt revealed far too much of my bosom. I wished he wouldn't look at me with such obvious pleasure.

"Where . . . where have you brought me?" My voice seemed not my own, and because he'd just admitted having to do with a piracy raid of sorts, I guessed that he indeed was a pirate himself. Had he raided Columb Manor and left all I knew in total ruin? Such things were not uncommon on the coast of Cornwall, or so I had often heard Melly say, and I could believe it now.

"We are on the coast of Brittany, Mademoiselle Columb. But do let us eat first, *s'il vous plaît.*" He held out the chair, his eyebrows tilted above the dark eyes. "All this we can discuss after our meal."

I relented and moved slowly across the room, wary of the man but knowing it was useless to pretend I wasn't famished. I took the chair he held, and when I sat down, he turned and took the silver goblets from the cabinet, as well as two plates and a tall silver flagon. He poured red wine into each goblet and passed one to me. Then he sat down across from me.

The sun, now flaming in the west, poured into the room and touched his black hair with reddish tints. I noticed coppery lights in his mustache as well, and I looked into the golden brown eyes which were on mine. I felt the warmth of his gaze like a caress, moving over my face and throat and bosom. I had every reason to fear this man, and I was confused as to why he was being so considerate after raiding my home and perhaps even killing my brother. . . . I closed my mind to the ugly fears and possibilities that lurked there, not able to cope with them.

He lifted the covers from the trays, and I nearly fainted from hunger at the sight of the deep brown roasted chicken. He laughed. "So. Jock has outdone himself in favor of our guest aboard

L'Angélique. He would be very sad if we wasted his excellent cuisine, I think."

There was a salad of greens lightly flavored with garlic and oil and lemon; a thick wedge of cheese, creamy yellow, with huge golden oranges, a large crusty loaf of the bread I'd smelled earlier, hidden under a rough blue and white cloth in a basket.

The Frenchman—I still did not know his name, for I could not be sure he was the Marquis de Rouvroy—cut it first with his knife and passed a thick slice to me; then he filled our plates, and it was all I could do to keep from falling upon it and wolfing it down. For a long time we both ate in silence, sipping the dry wine, eating until our hunger passed, and only then did we sit back, comfortable. I was certain it was the most delicious food I had ever eaten. The wine made my head light, and I felt rather giddy, but I had a sense of well-being as I watched him refill our goblets. Then he took an orange from the bowl and began to peel it, and I was fascinated by those long slender brown fingers skillfully stripping away the skin.

"Are you the captain of this ship, monsieur?" I asked, finding my tongue at last.

"Oui, mademoiselle, oui." His voice was low and pleasant, and it was hard for me to understand that he could be as brutally cruel as I'd seen him.

"Why did you bring me here?" I was suddenly conscious of a dryness on my lips, and I ran my tongue lightly over them. "My—brother. What—" I could not trust my voice then, for no matter how polite he was being, I knew behind it all lay an ulterior motive. I tried to piece it together, but I could not. I met my captor's eyes with my own wide ones, perhaps filled with fear, certainly with bewilderment.

Nothing in his expression betrayed what he was thinking, but his eyes darkened as he said, "You must not be frightened of me, Mademoiselle Columb. I did not murder your brother, although he deserves it; he was merely hit on the head and left in his study, to be found by the faithful servants of Columb Manor."

"But why, monsieur? Why . . . this?" I gestured vaguely with my hand, knowing he would understand.

Carefully he sectioned the orange, and with deliberate coolness he placed several portions in my plate, and then lifted his goblet to finish the wine.

"Has your brother ever mentioned the name of Rouvroy, or the Château de Rouvroy to you, mademoiselle?" His eyes regarded me with a cool calculation, and I was frightened.

So there it was. Rouvroy. The locket inside my pocket suddenly scorched against my thigh like fire, and I touched it with my hand. But I said truthfully, "No, monsieur. My brother never once mentioned that name. Should he have done so?" I lifted my brows.

"He did not tell you of his former life? Did you not know that he was an English spy, working along with the Royalists for my country? That he was a leader of a renegade band who called themselves the *Chouans,* the Brittany peasants who fought valiantly against the New Republic of France?"

I was silent; of course I had not known such things, but what was I supposed to say? How could I defend my brother when I knew nothing of his life during those years he'd been working for the War Department. What could I deny, even?

"You do not speak, mademoiselle." He was almost accusing.

"I could not know of what my brother was doing during years that I was but a . . . schoolgirl. That was long ago, in the past. What can it have to do with the Château de Rouvroy? Is that . . . your name?"

I saw the deep flush of his skin, and the sudden satirical curl of his lips. The locket belonged to this noble family, and I knew for certain that what was happening now was linked in some subtle way to the past through that locket.

"I am Jean de Rouvroy, the Marquis de Rouvroy, mademoiselle." He said it with a fierce pride, and I felt stung by it, as if he meant that I should bow to him.

Had Neville lied to me about the locket, then? I could not think so—I *dared* not think so! Yet I recalled the words this Frenchman had spoken to Neville in his study: *"I will not forget Danielle. You are the Englishman who robbed her and betrayed my parents!"*

Before I could think of anything to say, he spoke. "Your brother called himself Marc Renoire. He came to the château, befriending my people, especially my father and mother who had just returned secretly from their forced exile to help in the cause. No one ever knew that my father returned, mademoiselle; the château, as it is now, was restored to the family through my uncle, who, safe in exile through the war, returned only when he accepted the new order and was given a free pardon from General Bonaparte. The title and the château are mine, but my uncle is there in my place, everyone believing that he is my own father."

"You confuse me, monsieur. How can your uncle fool everyone so?"

"They were identical twins. Even I was fooled for a short while."

"Where was your father? Why did his brother take his place?"

"My father was killed at Quiberon Bay. He was betrayed, and he died like a hunted animal, with no pride, nor did anyone know that it was he, the Marquis de Rouvroy."

I frowned, deeply interested but puzzled. "How? Why?"

"At the first outbreak of the Revolution, my father and mother went into exile at my uncle's insistence. But my father was a patriot, loving France more than anything. He held liberal views, but he went into exile; I suppose in a way that saved the château from the National Guard and the mobs. Rouvroy is on the coast, not far from here, built right on the cliffs, impregnable by any sea invasion. The sea wind always blows there, the smell of salt is in the air, and gulls cry. . . ."

I thought of Columb Manor, and my heart

ached with longing and tears filled my eyes. I was glad he was not looking at me.

"They went to England, but returned just after the king was tried for treason. He and my mother were leaders of a group of Royalists fighting against the New Republic in Brittany, incognito, of course, for it was very dangerous to be known as a nobleman, much less the Marquis and Marquise de Rouvroy. For a time they were successful; having the Vendeans to support them, they fought heroically along with the devout Catholic peasants and nobility. It was a formidable insurrection against the French revolutionary government, and they soon controlled most of Brittany. The English, of course, had supported it all, sending in their agents, gold, guns, and ammunition."

He stood up and walked over to stare out the window, one arm leaning on the casement.

"What happened then?" I found myself asking.

"The great plan of landing the Royalist émigrés at Quiberon failed; General Hoche was waiting for them. It had fallen on my parents to try to warn the ship's landing party, but they failed, along with the Englishman. They escaped that massacre only to be betrayed later. *Someone* let it be known where their hideout was. They were caught in a church on that same dark night, and were shot at dawn, along with five others. Only the Englishman escaped. As I have said, it was not known that those who were shot were my parents, and even my cousin Maurice, who brags about his winning favors from the Corsican in his glorious army, doesn't know that it's his own father and not mine who returned from exile with that pardon, lands restored and all for my sake, of course." He spoke with such bitter contempt, that I couldn't help but see that this had wounded him deeply.

"Where were you during all of it, monsieur?" My voice was low, soft.

"At the outbreak of the Revolution, I was sent into exile, learning my trade on my father's ship. It was a form of exile, anyway. Unlike Maurice, who was sent to Switzerland with his youngest sister, I was given a chance to fight my battles on the Indian Ocean, instead of facing a guillotine, and this was what my father and mother wanted above all things—that their son and heir should be safe to take an empty title when and if the New Republic should emerge. I returned at the highlight of it all, just long enough to find that my parents were living like hunted animals, hiding their identity, starving themselves to fight for a dead king."

"But all was not lost," I couldn't help saying. "I mean, you have the château they fought to save for you, do you not? And your uncle was willing to see that it was all regained. Was it damaged? The château, I mean."

He shook his head. "No. Only a miracle prevented it."

I thought of the locket and of the picture of the young man inside it, and gazed at this older man, hardened by bitterness and a hate for one Englishman who he believed betrayed his parents and sent them to their deaths. "How old were you then, monsieur?"

He turned to look darkly at me. "Old enough to have taken my place with them, Mademoiselle Columb. A twenty-two-year-old man should have been fighting for the cause with them, but they would not hear of it. I had to creep out like a thief myself, leaving them to their fate. I could not even take the time to find my sister who had been allowed to take part all those years, for the noose was being tightened and escape routes by sea were being watched. I slipped *L'Angélique* out in a thick fog right under the nose of General Hoche's guns. And I never saw my parents again."

"But how do you explain your mother's absence as the marquise in the château now, monsieur? And your uncle's wife?"

"My uncle's wife died in the birth of their youngest daughter. And it was explained that my mother took ill and died in exile. It was easy then for my uncle to return as the bereaved husband and Marquis de Rouvroy. My father and my uncle were remarkably identical; Honoré five minutes older than Henri. And so it is. My parents are dead, betrayed by an Englishman who called himself Marc Renoire and that man is Neville Columb." His mouth was brutal, his words filled with malice toward my own brother.

"How can you be so sure when you were not there, monsieur? Why would an Englishman betray someone he was closely working with if he was an agent for their cause, especially at the last moment?"

He shrugged. "Who knows why a man will betray another? Spies are men, after all; in war there is anger and jealousy, and those who live so dan-

gerously close to life and death have many reasons
for betrayal. We cannot know, can we? But I know
it was Neville Columb, your brother, mademoiselle, who betrayed my parents that night. He was
captured, but because he was English and revealed
the hideout at the church, that was enough, and
he escaped to safety, leaving them to die in their
own spilled blood." The accusation stunned me.
This man hated my brother.

Appalled, I cried out, "How can you be sure?
There must have been others who could have betrayed your parents! How can you justify your
condemnation of someone you did not know?" I
couldn't help my outburst of anger in defense of
my brother.

"It was my uncle who knew your brother, and it
was he who finally told me the story, from beginning to end." His voice was quiet but hard, and it
took my breath from me.

My mind was whirling. That my brother could
betray anyone was unthinkable. It all seemed to
add up, but I would not accept it. Never! Yet I
was haunted by those words Jean de Rouvroy had
spoken to my brother in that last dramatic
moment at Columb Manor; they seemed to ring
out in vivid clarity now.

"Monsieur—" I stopped, yet knew I had to find
the courage to ask. "Who is . . . Danielle?"

His dark eyes blazing, he demanded, "Where
did you hear that name, mademoiselle?" He took
one long stride and stood over me, his hands
clenched.

I swallowed hard, close to panic. "You spoke the
name to my brother, monsieur. You said you'd not

forget Danielle. Did my brother know her?" I could hardly get the words out, and I knew mixed emotions, for I couldn't erase the memory of Neville's tormented face, nor could I ignore the yellowed note secreted inside the locket.

I looked up into a face black with pain and hate, and I shrank inside with fear.

"Danielle is my sister," he said darkly. "She had a lover whose identity she would not disclose to my parents. She bore his child six months after he left her as bait in the plot to outwit General Hoche's company of men that night of the intended invasion. He did not return for her, but left her at the mercy of those beasts! No! I will not forget what he did to her! He will pay for that!"

I thought I saw it all clearly now; he'd abducted me to get revenge on the man who had caused his sister—Danielle of the picture and note—untold pain at the hands of her captors.

He turned back to the window, but he was restless now, and he seemed to be making up his mind about something. I began to feel uneasy. Then, with his back to me, he said in that arrogant voice, "I will take you to the château tonight, Mademoiselle Columb. I will present you to my uncle, whom you will know as my father, the Marquis de Rouvroy. You must give me your word that you will not try to escape, and I will see that you are treated with respect. I will bring you as . . . an impoverished English lady whom I rescued from the hands of Barbary pirates in the Straits, and because you have no means of support, you can be the governess to my niece, who needs to learn English. That will be a way of explaining your sudden appearance. But you must remember this, mademoiselle, and remember it well. You are my prisoner, and if you cannot go along with my scheme, then I will lock you in one of the dungeons beneath the château, and you will never see your brother again! Do not forget it for one instant!" It was unmistakably a threat, and meant to frighten me.

"But . . . why, monsieur? What can you hope to gain by holding me against my will? You cannot mean to hold me for . . . ransom?" My heart was pounding furiously, my face hot with indignation.

"Your brother will know the answer to that, mademoiselle. It is he who will pay the price to have his only sister back."

He turned then and strode over to the bed. He brought out my red cloak and held it out. "If you are ready, we shall take the boat ashore now. I had one of my men pack for you some of your own clothes while you were dancing in the hall last night. That will be easier to explain, and I'm sure you will feel more at home with your own gowns. It will be quite cold on shore, as it is approaching night, and we have a very rough walk ahead of us, so please put on your cloak."

My mind was racing as I realized he had planned this all in advance, had sailed to Cornwall and found Columb Manor, and had moved in like a thief, or the pirate that he surely was, waiting for the right moment. I had no doubt that my brother, and Cameron too, would come after me. Immediately! But—what was the price this man was exacting from Neville?

I stood up, met his eyes, inscrutable now with

calculation, and I knew a sense of helpless fury as he placed the cloak around my shoulders. Then he opened the door and called for Jock, who appeared immediately. Jock ran to do his master's bidding, to get my valise and lower it into the boat alongside the ship. I followed Jean de Rouvroy through a narrow galleyway and up some steps onto the deck. Strange men with hard brown faces, rough seamen, were there, and turned to watch me with undue interest, I thought, and when their captain spoke to them, two ran over to the side and lowered the rope ladder over the deck rail. One sailor went over the side carrying my valise, and Jean followed him, giving instructions to another sailor to assist me from the deck.

I took the first unsteady step, my cloak and skirts billowing out around me in the wind. I missed a rung and hung there for a moment suspended, my hands clutching the rope for dear life lest I should fall in that water between the ship and the boat. I was frightened, but more than that I was embarrassed, knowing that those eyes above me were watching with pleasure.

Suddenly I felt two strong arms gripping me around my waist, and I was lifted bodily off the ladder. For one instant my cheek brushed closely against the warm, bronzed face of Jean de Rouvroy. The sensation was like a flame coursing through every fiber of my being; it was stunning, and it left me oddly weak so that when he set me down I was trembling.

Above us the cry went up, *"Voilà! Enchanté!"* My face flamed as I looked up to see the faces of the crew waving at their captain and whistling.

My captor did not speak as we were rowed toward the shore. He had put on his coat, and when we reached the gray stone quay, he jumped out first and tied the rope in place. He helped me from the boat and took my valise from the sailor, who remained in the boat. Then Jean de Rouvroy gestured for me to follow him along the quay and I pulled my cloak around me as we walked toward the shelter of shadowy trees.

We stood among the trees for a moment, and then I heard what I thought was a screech owl and, startled, I shuddered. For within the trees, the dusk had deepened and shadows were almost black now. I heard the screech owl closer now and suddenly a man appeared. He approached Jean de Rouvroy with a smile on his wild looking face, and the two men clasped hands firmly.

"Jean! *Mon Dieu*, it is good to see you again!" He laughed, throwing his head back.

"*Voilà*, Nicolas, *mon ami*," Jean said. I noticed the easiness between the two men as they talked in low tones, stepping aside from me. I, however, was uneasy, for it now occurred to me that I was on French soil for the first time, and a captive at that! I stared at them, Jean's back to me, as they talked. Then all at once Jean turned and introduced me to this man.

"Nicolas Cottereau, this is Mademoiselle Columb from England. She is my fiancée, and will be staying at the château for a while. Tamar, my friend and compatriot, Nicolas Cottereau."

This announcement was so utterly unexpected that I felt myself go pale.

"*Vraiment?* This comes as a surprise, Jean. Your

father, le Marquis, will no doubt be as surprised too, not to mention *la jeune* Mademoiselle Charette!" But he laughed and took my hand and kissed it. "*Mais oui, enchanté,* Mademoiselle Columb. Jean is very lucky indeed, I can see that. Congratulations, *mon vieux*." He winked at Jean and slapped him on the back.

Jean did not laugh with him, nor did he elaborate now that the introduction was over. He hurried the man on to his business or whatever it was he had been doing when we arrived, and Nicolas turned once again to me, smiled with that wide mouth and teeth flashing in the dark face and said, "*Au revoir,* mademoiselle, I leave you now. But may we meet again, *n'est-ce pas?*"

"Of course, Monsieur Cottereau. *Au revoir.*"

"*Bon.*" And he disappeared among the trees.

Jean took my arm. "We must hurry on now. Follow me closely. The path is quite difficult, for it is rough in places."

I bit my lip and did not move, but said in an angry voice, "Monsieur, why did you introduce me to that man as your fiancée? I thought you had decided on something quite different, and I must know where I stand, monsieur. I will not budge from here until I know what you have in mind!" I was adamant.

He had already taken a few steps away from me, and now he turned and walked back slowly, standing over me and looking down into my face. "There will be fewer questions asked if I present you as my fiancée. I realized that the moment Nicolas appeared." He hesitated. "We need only pretend, mademoiselle, for the time you are to be at the château. You will be accepted as such, have no fear." His words were cool and calculating, all-knowing. "Now we must hurry on before the gates are closed. I do not want to arouse the whole place." He started away from me, and because I could do nothing to change what was happening to me, I had to follow or be left behind.

As it turned out, two hours later, with a golden moon rising out of the night sky, I saw the Château de Rouvroy for the first time. We had walked in silence most of the way on a treacherous path, and suddenly the jagged fangs of the rocks rose up from the sea, looking as if they lifted the castle out of that foaming water, holding it, the gray-green mass of dark walls and ramparts with two square towers bathed in that hazy nocturnal light.

He stopped, stared at it, and I thought it the most romantic sight I had ever seen. It seemed impossible that such a lovely place was to be my prison. *"Le Château de Rouvroy,"* the young marquis said softly, almost as if to himself. "It's . . . beautiful," I found myself whispering. "Almost . . . ethereal."

"It is always like this by moonlight, beautifully remote. It cannot be approached by sea here, and that is why the ship had to be anchored down the coast. We have taken this route because of certain precautions of the new order; General Bonaparte is having the coast watched closely, it seems." He said dryly, "He is not welcome here, you see, not in Brittany. But he doesn't trust us, and he is right about that." I thought I saw a gleam of contempt in his expression.

"I take it then that you do not hold with the New Republic, monsieur. Are you a Royalist like your father was?"

He turned to look at me, and for a moment I believed his expression softened. "I love France, Mademoiselle Tamar," and the way he spoke my name made it sound enchanting. "I believe in her, and in her future. But where does it lie? Certainly not with an upstart Corsican who dreams of being made an emperor! If men like Nicolas and his father and uncles who fought and died heroically here in Brittany continue to stir up courage in other families, we may know the answer. Surely enough blood has been spilled in the cause of liberty, but what should we follow, if not our hearts?"

I was certain he was speaking to himself as well as to me, and in that moment I could have almost forgotten that he was taking me to his château to hold me for ransom.

"Are you telling me that there are still those who would fight against General Bonaparte, even as it was . . . then?"

He looked at me, saying nothing for a long moment. "Nicolas Cottereau and his uncle belong to one of our finest families here on our coast. His father fought side by side with my parents. The *Chouans* were the *Chevaliers de Foi,* most noble in the cause for freedom, and Nicolas has not forgotten, nor have I."

"Did his father know about . . . your father, the marquis?"

65

"I am not certain, you see. The *Chouans* kept so secret that none knew their faces. But Nicolas does not know. Of that I am sure."

I shivered suddenly, and he saw it. "We must go inside. Once again I must warn you of the consequences, mademoiselle. You are my prisoner; I shall say I rescued you from your burning ship at the hands of Barbary pirates, and that you are now my fiancée. To give you something worthwhile to do, you are willing to act as governess for my small niece. Is it all clear and understood?"

"I have no choice, have I, Monsieur le Marquis?"

"Yes." A ghost of a smile played about his mouth. "You may object and then I will take you to the dungeon right now. I have ways of dealing with those who cross me, Mademoiselle Tamar. Never doubt that."

"So you have warned me, monsieur!" I said testily, angry that he could do as he wished with me, and I met his eyes with a defiant glare.

"Just as long as you remember it." The coldness in his manner frightened me, and we turned to walk down a slope through a grove of trees, and came alongside high stone walls, entering through a wide archway into the courtyard. A lantern glowed above the stables, and a man came out, followed by a huge black Doberman that bounded out and at once came up to Jean. "Héro! How goes it, old boy?" Dog and master greeted each other fondly. The other man stood by watching, a grin of welcome on his weathered face.

Then somehow we were within the house. All around us doors opened, and lights flickered from candles held high, and the next thing I knew was the flurry of vivid red skirts as an exquisite young woman flung herself into Jean's arms.

"Jean! You've come back! Oh, you've come back to your loving Charette! I knew you would—I just knew it. I know your papa will be very happy that you have come! He has been so upset in these last weeks!" She kissed him warmly, and while they were locked in each other's arms I was filled with an amazing envy.

What should it matter? I told myself coldly. The man certainly meant nothing to me! It would be amusing to watch how he would explain a fiancée to this charming young woman. I felt I could understand now the surprise with which Nicolas Cottereau had spoken when Jean had introduced me as his fiancée.

Jean put her from him, not unkindly, but I fancied I saw a slow flush stain his face, for the woman would not be put off so easily, so he said, "It's good to see you looking so pretty, Charette. My little cousin, grown up into a lovely young woman." His eyes caught mine over her head of shining black hair curled in wispy ringlets.

"We can be married now, Jean, can we not? Maurice says we cannot because we are cousins, but he doesn't know everything—" She stopped then and whirled around, and as the round, sparkling brown eyes rested on me, she gave a little gasp. "Who is she, Jean? Why have you brought her here?" she pouted. She was hardly more than seventeen, and I could see she was the adored—and probably spoiled—daughter of a man who tragically had to pretend he was her uncle.

Jean seemed unduly embarrassed by her outburst and didn't know what to say in the moment of it, but he was suddenly rescued when another door opened and a tall dark man came out, elegant in black evening dress, and as distinctively aristocratic as Jean de Rouvroy was. The resemblance between the two men was striking.

"Jean!" the man exclaimed, surprised, and hurried over to embrace him heartily. "*Mon Dieu,* I thought I heard a commotion and came out to see what it was." His voice was thick and deep, and I believed I heard pride in it for this younger man. It could have been his own father, I thought, already stunned by the amazing resemblance. He was still handsomely virile, and I decided this would be what Jean would be like when he reached this age. Tall, lean, with piercing dark eyes and graying hair, this man was undeniably of the old nobility of Bourbon France. And Jean was like him in every way.

"I'm glad to see you've returned safely. The situation here has been very tense since you left us. And *L'Angélique?*" He lifted dark brows. "She is safe?"

"*Mais oui,*" Jean assured me. I glanced at the young girl, who, forgotten in this greeting, now turned her lovely face up to both men, her hand going through Jean's arm.

"Uncle Honoré," she said sweetly, "Jean has brought a . . . guest with him. He must introduce her." I had stood in the background before, but now all eyes turned on me; Jean moved away from his cousin and stood at my side.

"Father, may I present Mademoiselle Tamar Columb? She is my fiancée, and I have brought her here under your protection. Tamar, this is *mon père,* Monsieur Honoré de Rouvroy, the marquis. You are safe here." I believed his eyes were glinting wickedly with his own deceit, and I could have slapped him for it, knowing my color was extremely high resulting from the uncomfortable position he'd forced me into.

The lifted eyebrows, the dark probing eyes on my own revealed complete surprise, but in a second the brief shock was gone as the older man took my hand in his, bringing it to his lips to kiss it.

"Vraiment? C'est magnifique, Jean! You are one for surprises, eh? Mademoiselle," he touched my cheek with a warm kiss of welcome. *"Enchanté, enchanté.* Welcome to the château, *ma chère.* Let me congratulate you both, and wish you happiness here with us."

"Merci beaucoup, Monsieur le Marquis," I managed to say, blushing furiously under those penetrating eyes. He still kept my hand imprisoned in his own strong one.

"Tell me, Jean. Where did you find such a lovely young woman as Mademoiselle Tamar? And without our knowing!" The dark eyes glowed with what I deemed to be pleasure at this sudden surprise.

Jean laughed, and I turned to stare at him. "Tamar is English. I found her on the deck of her burning ship, just off the Barbary Coast, and came to her rescue before her captors could enslave her. I fear she may need much protection, Father, for my fiancée still suffers from fears of being abducted." I had the urge to laugh, and would have done so had I not been so angry. Of all the insufferable, odious creatures! But I had to give him credit, for his cunning guile had convinced his uncle.

"*Voilà! Tant pis,*" the marquis said softly, and looked at me as if I were indeed a treasure stolen from those imaginary pirates in this masquerade. "So you have come to the château. Of course we shall make you feel protected, *ma chère* Mademoiselle Tamar. We welcome you with open arms, eh what, *ma petite* Charette?"

He turned to his own daughter then. She looked hurt and bewildered, her great eyes going from Jean to the marquis, resting on my face with hate. With a small gasp of that pain of shock, she turned and ran from the room, disappearing through doors that she slammed behind her.

The marquis shrugged. "You must forgive Charette, mademoiselle. She is young and fancies herself in love—not for the first time, of course, but this time it is with Jean. I will speak to her." He spoke not unkindly, but affectionately as a father would, and I could see clearly that he was disturbed.

"Of course," I said.

"I think you had better follow her now, Father," he said. "I will look after Tamar. I'm sure Madame Hortense will have rooms ready, and I shall take my fiancée up to her."

The marquis agreed to this, turned to me and bowed. "Then I will bid you good-night and we shall talk in the morning."

"You must be exhausted," Jean said when we were alone. "Come with me." And without another word he moved toward a door and I followed him. We went up a wide flight of stairs, taking candles to light our way through a labyrinth of corridors, their rich paneling decorated with splendid paintings, and past lovely windows of stained glass. I followed Jean along a passage and up some stairs to yet another floor, and down this corridor to what seemed to be the very end of the château, and he stopped in front of a door. As he opened it, he turned to me.

"You will be safe here, I believe. I am just down the hall. I will have a *fille de chambre* come to you, but I think it would be wise not to disturb the housekeeper tonight. *Entrez-vous, s'il vous plaît*, mademoiselle." He stepped aside, close to me as I passed him. So he meant to stay near at hand, to watch me, I thought, and my eyes almost smarted with tears.

But I was not prepared for the room I entered: the stark whiteness of the walls glistening even in candlelight. It was small, with only a wooden crucifix to decorate its walls, and over the bed was a white woolen spread. The carpet was a dull brown; there was a small table and chair, a fireplace, and a curtained-off alcove which served as a dressing room and bath—a *garde-robe,* like in a medieval fortress. Windows in thick-set embrasures were flung open to bring in the salty smell of sea air, and the brown velvet curtains were looped back with round wooden rings hooked on iron knobs. Moonlight flooded in, pure and unreal.

Jean pulled a tasseled rope near the door and then placed my valise down. Then, seeing my astonishment, he said, "It is not our best salon, mademoiselle, but you will be safe here." He kept repeating *safe,* and I suppose I was at his mercy. He lingered, walking over to the window, and stared out, almost as if to check escape routes. "Yes. You will be safe here. Ah," he turned, hearing a sound outside the door, "here is the *fille de chambre* now. It is Lili." He smiled rather too familiarly, I thought contemptuously, at the rather pretty maid who entered. After a few rapid instructions about bringing up hot water and some light refreshment for the poor English mademoiselle, the young girl, rosy-cheeked and bright-eyed, curtsied and hurried out. Jean winked at me, boldly, conspiracy darkening his eyes.

I understood it all very well now. He would play his little games, even with the servants, and I was to be his pawn, thrust back and forth across whatever board he chose to use! My face flamed with this sudden revelation.

"You must come and look out the window, mademoiselle. I know you will be impressed with the view from here. See?" He went again to the window and beckoned me, for I had not moved since I first came inside.

Reluctantly I went over to the window and stared out, feeling much too close to this man, for the embrasure was barely wide enough for two people. Far below were those jagged rocks rising eerily from a pale, frothy sea. A sudden dizziness overwhelmed me and I stepped back, caught from falling only by my captor's strong hand.

"It is quite breathtaking, *n'est-ce pas?* A long,

long drop down." His face was close and my throat tightened. "You cannot escape me, *ma chère* Tamar. So do not even try." He had gripped my wrists with fingers like a band of steel, and I almost cried out in pain before he released them.

He did not leave me until the maid, Lili, hurried back, and only when the hot water was brought along with a small tray of food and drink, did the maid withdraw. Then Jean de Rouvroy leaned over me and touched my cheek with his fingers. I drew back as if I'd been struck by a lightning bolt. My skin felt scorched, and the expression in his eyes was that of satanic satisfaction.

"I will see you in the morning, and I will personally give you a tour of the Château de Rouvroy. Good-night." And he left me, closing the door firmly. It was when I heard the key in the lock turn that I knew I had been locked in, and that I had hardly spoken a word to him in my defense!

Never was I so angry as I was at that moment. Staring at the heavy wooden door, I seethed with that anger, and when I went over to the alcove and jerked back the curtain, I ran a practiced eye over the inadequate furnishings. My anger cooled as I realized nothing could be gained by it, and exhaustion overwhelmed me. I removed my cloak and hung it on one of the pegs at hand, then took off my gown and stepped into the hip-bath which was already filled with warm water.

As I bathed, scrubbing away the weariness as well as the travel stains, I tried to reason things out, but I could not, and I couldn't help the tears that came as I thought of Neville and the home I might never see again. I did not think of Cameron, but only of my brother and the pain I'd seen in his face.

What would he do when he was able to revive himself? And what were Jean's plans for that "exact payment?" A wave of terror washed over me. He wanted Neville here! To fight in a duel? I could not know, but it caused a deep dread inside my heart. He had baited my brother by taking me by force in front of him, so that Neville would come after me!

By the time I was out of the bath and in my own chemise I'd dug out of the valise, I was trembling in fear. I drank some hot chocolate, knowing I would not sleep this night. My thoughts were filled with sorrow and anger and a thousand unanswered questions. . . .

When I'd snuffed out the candles, moonlight lay like pink down in the room, and I found my way to that window again and stared out. I did not look down again, however, and turned back into the room and went to bed. As I lay down, the rhythmic sound of the sea pounding against the rocks could have put me to sleep had I not remembered Danielle, Jean de Rouvroy's sister. Something in the back of my mind seemed to explode. I sat up. Danielle. Of course! The note inside the locket!

What had Jean said of her? That she'd had a lover whose identity she wouldn't disclose to her parents, except that he was an Englishman. She had borne his child six months after he'd left her as bait in the plot to root out General Hoche's men. The Englishman had not returned for her, but had left her at the mercy of those . . . beasts!

And he had accused Neville of being that Englishman.

3

I hurried from the bed and found my lovely ball gown where I'd hung it as best I could beside the cloak, and with a trembling hand and a tight little knot in my throat I took the locket from that hidden pocket. It lay heavy in my hands, and I relit one of the candles I'd blown out so that I could study again what was inside. Carefully I removed the picture from its gold tongs and brought out the yellowed note.

"Unless I am mistaken, I do not doubt that you will come. Danielle."

Had that person failed to keep the rendezvous? Had it been my brother? If it were not, then how on earth could such a locket as this one ever have come to Columb Manor? But Neville had denied ever seeing this locket and, what was more important, I believed him.

The pain of recognition in Neville's face when the Frenchman had mentioned Danielle, however, kept returning to my mind, and I was haunted by it with excruciating anguish which I found almost unbearable.

I studied the picture of the young woman in the locket. She might have been my own age at that time. Certainly she was Jean's sister. Was it possible, then, that Neville was that Englishman Jean believed him to be? I dared not think it. She had a child, he'd said. And if what he'd said was true, then that child—Jean's niece—would be my niece too! Neville's . . . Oh, dear God!

I shook my head in disbelief, stunned. Why hadn't Neville told me? And what had happened to Danielle? Had she given birth to her child and perished afterward, as Jean's words almost implied she had? "I will not forget Danielle," he'd said. But her child lived. I was to act as her governess.

A dim memory touched me. When Neville had come to take me away from Miss Rochelle's school that year, he'd returned from his long absence like a man haunted, as if he'd come out of a long illness, desperate, and he'd taken me with him everywhere. How right Marietta Pennland had been when she'd spoken of his deep sadness. It must be true. But it couldn't be. So much of the story was still unknown to me.

And Jean de Rouvroy was using me to draw Neville back to Brittany. He wanted to even the score, to get revenge. I was frightened not only for Neville, but for myself.

I returned to bed, taking the locket with me, not knowing what I should do with it. There was a connection somewhere, something explaining why it had been lost—and found—at Columb Manor, and if Neville had not brought it there, then who else could be responsible?

In spite of myself, I slept that night only to be wakened by the *fille de chambre,* Lili, who was shaking my shoulder.

"Mademoiselle. *S'il vous plaît,* you must wake up and come with me at once." I opened my eyes and saw her merry eyes dancing on my face. It seemed quite early.

Startled, I sat up. "What is wrong? What's happened?"

She had the audacity to laugh. "Nothing has happened, mademoiselle. But you are to come with me. I am to take you to the boudoir. See? I have already removed your things. Please put on your wrapper and come at once. Monsieur will be very angry with me if you do not."

I frowned. "But surely you jest. It is far too early to be traipsing about."

"*Mais oui,* mademoiselle, it is early, of course, but that is why you must come with me and now. *S'il vous plaît!*" She stood back, holding out the wrapper, and looked at me expectantly. I believe it startled her that I had been speaking French back to her easily enough, although her dialect was quite Breton and a bit hard to grasp.

I pulled myself out of the bed, and as I did so, I saw the locket on the sheets where I'd lain. Smitten with guilt, I grabbed it, thankful for the dark curtain of my long hair then to hide my face from the searching eyes of this maid. That she had seen the locket there was no doubt, but I wondered if she would know it. Judging from her age—which was not more than sixteen or seventeen—I guessed that she could not have seen it when it was in Danielle's possession. But all the same, I didn't want anyone to know I possessed such a piece of jewelry. It was a sort of talisman for the condemnation already heaped upon Neville, and I had to steady myself as the damning evidence flooded my mind.

"Very well, Lili," I said, standing up and allowing her to help me with my wrapper. "But it is most unusual, *n'est-ce pas,* to move a guest about like this so early in the morning?" I looked out the window and saw the sky was faintly tinged with pink; it was barely daybreak.

I followed Lili out of the room and down the dim corridor to another wing of the house. We walked up steps and came to a spacious corridor with gilt-framed mirrors and portraits, and I noticed a table with a bowl of flowers on its polished surface. Across from this was a door that Lili opened, and she hurried in ahead of me.

The room was a far cry from the little white cell Jean had put me in last night. This was indeed what one might have expected in a château. The boudoir, as Lili called it, was all pale blue and rose; the bed was draped in pink satin coverlets and sheets, a pale blue Persian carpet covered the polished floors, and blue curtains hung at the wide windows and around the enormous fourposter. Adjoining this room was a smaller one which, in comparison to my own at Columb Manor, was like a salon itself. My clothes were already unpacked, my toilette ready for me.

I was astounded. "Did Monsieur de Rouvroy give you instructions to bring me here?" I asked Lili. I knew my voice was sharp, for the poor girl looked at me with uncertainty.

"*Oui.*" I saw her face was flushed, and I guessed then that he had bribed her to do this. But for what reason? I asked myself. I turned my back on the girl and went to the windows, drawing back the curtains, while my heart seemed to beat in my throat. He had meant to frighten me . . . locking me in, threatening me with a cell in his dungeons if I didn't cower and obey him! What angered me was that I had believed him, when he and this *fille de chambre* were using my fear of him to amuse themselves. I could barely control my temper, and I wished for a means of retaliation.

I was not aware the maid had left, it was only when I heard the closing of the door that I turned and saw Lili entering with a tray upon which there was a silver pot and a cup and saucer. I assumed then I was to be given special consideration this morning. The marquis had made his point.

She looked abashed, a little frightened too, as she set the tray down and began to pour hot chocolate for me. "Madame Hortense will be coming in very soon, mademoiselle. She is very upset that she was not informed of your arrival last night, for she is the châtelaine. She will want to see for herself that you are comfortable."

"I see. Then I was given the wrong room last night, Lili?"

She lowered her eyes. She was a pretty girl, I thought, and would be easily persuaded, perhaps with a few stolen kisses in the corridor, by such a rogue as the young marquis to play a part in making his fiancée feel she was his prisoner *de l'amour.*

"*Oui,*" she said, embarrassed.

"You have seen monsieur this morning then? And he . . . persuaded you to hurry me and my clothes into this room, so Madame Hortense would not know that I had been given . . . the wrong room?"

She looked so startled that I had discovered their little scheme that I might have burst out laughing had I not been so angry. "*Oui,* mademoiselle. Monsieur thought only to . . . protect you."

"You are to be my maid then?" She nodded. "Very well, Lili," I said, taking the cup of chocolate from her. "You may begin by preparing my bath, and then see to my clothes. They are in such a state that it will take you days to press out the wrinkles." I thought of Jean's man grabbing and stuffing my clothes into my valise, and I knew a sudden revulsion at the thought that a Frenchman had gone through my room! "After you have done this, I will choose what gown I will wear for the morning. I would like my breakfast brought to me, and I do not wish to be disturbed."

I would play Monsieur Jean de Rouvroy's little game; I would assume the role as well as take the rights which a true fiancée should expect. He would learn that his scheme could work both ways—for him, and for me.

When Madame Hortense, the châtelaine of the château, came in to introduce herself a short time later, I could see that she found nothing remiss;

eagle-eyed, to be sure, thus increasing Lili's anxieties, she was nonetheless pleased that I was comfortable. She seemed satisfied that Lili was doing for me properly, and she herself took my gowns in hand and said, "I will see that they are like new, mademoiselle." She eyed the crushed ball gown, exclaimed over its exquisite beauty, and took it with her. Evidently she had been told about the rescue from the burning decks of an English ship set upon by a band of pirates, and I was beginning to believe it myself.

Mid-morning, I was summoned to the *grande salle*. "*S'il vous plaît,* mademoiselle. The marquis wishes your presence. I am to take you there," Lili informed me as she bustled into the room.

I followed her through a maze of corridors, down beautifully carved staircases and into the *grande salle.* Nothing like this existed either at Columb Manor or Penn Hall; it was as if I had stepped back in time to when the nobility truly flourished, and I caught my breath in sheer wonder.

The long windows opened onto a terrace, and from that terrace paths stretched into the small, boxed gardens, where rose trellises and arches hid little arbors. It was beautiful in the mellow light of late September sun.

The room was filled with mirrors and chairs covered in shades of blue and rose satin edged in gold, and echoing the very colors of the boudoir. The high ceiling was painted with cherubs and angels, and was incredibly impressive. I had time to glimpse a harpsichord in one corner of the room, and had a fleeting impression of Danielle playing that delightful instrument. I had to bring myself back to reality, however, for at the other end of the salon Jean awaited me.

Years afterward I would always remember the feeling I had as I stood there on that threshold; I could almost believe that I was indeed Jean de Rouvroy's fiancée and about to be presented to the small group on the other side of the room.

Jean hurried to greet me, and although his face was inscrutable, I glanced up into his eyes, smiling, taking his arm quite willingly and acting out the part he'd forced me to play.

"*Bonjour,* Tamar," he said in a low voice before we started toward the others. His eyes searched my face, and I fancied he seemed anxious, if not puzzled at my submission. This would be quite entertaining, I thought.

"Good morning . . . Jean," I said lingeringly, as if to hold him back from hurrying me into the company of the others.

But if I thought he would apologize for locking me in that little room last night, I was mistaken, for he did not. He looked excessively handsome in the dark brown velvet coat he wore this morning, the white frilled shirt beneath it accentuating his bronzed skin.

"My father wishes you to meet the others, Tamar," he said, "and perhaps you would allow me to escort you around the château afterward?" He lifted his brows, and that already familiar mocking expression came back into his face.

"The dungeons, no doubt?" I looked up at him so innocently that he turned red with anger and embarrassment. "But, the *fille de chambre* would help you, no doubt, persuaded by a few light kisses—"

He laughed then, throwing back his head, and looked down at me. I was sure of it then, and for some unknown reason I felt irritated, and I knew he saw that. My skin felt too hot for comfort, and I allowed him to take me to his uncle, another master of deceit.

That man greeted me warmly, affectionately, as if he had already accepted me into the family. He brought my hand up to his lips and kissed it in the old chevalier custom, his eyes smiling down into mine.

"*Mon Dieu,* but how radiant you are this morning, *ma chère* Tamar."

"*Merci,* monsieur," I said, matching his smile.

"Jean tells me that he placed you in the boudoir in the west wing. It was very wise of him, considering our limited staff these days. You were not frightened, were you? But you can be sure you are perfectly safe with us, *ma chère.*"

I laughed. "*Mais oui,* Monsieur le Marquis. But for Jean's consideration and close presence, I'm certain to have felt terrified! I felt . . . locked in, and very safe from those rogues Jean rescued me from!"

I glanced up into Jean's eyes, and I had the satisfaction of seeing them glitter with what I thought to be dissatisfaction; I gave him a wide, flashing smile and placed my hand possessively through his arm.

"We shall have a celebration to announce your engagement, if you want it known, Jean," the marquis said. He looked at the younger man for a sign of approval.

"It need not be so soon, Father. I believe Tamar wants to try to locate . . . a relative, before we set about with formal announcements. Is this not so, Tamar?"

"Your message was most likely received by now, Jean, and I suspect we shall be hearing from him shortly. You did say the Château de Rouvroy in Brittany, did you not? How could my brother fail to know where to find me if you gave him explicit directions?"

He was not jarred by my barbed remarks, but the marquis seemed quite amused. "*Voilà,* my two turtledoves," the marquis laughed, winking at me. "Just as you wish. But we shall have some small entertainment among us—a toast to congratulate you both."

"*Merci.* It is most thoughtful. I'm sure Tamar agrees," Jean said politely.

I lowered my eyes, lest the marquis should see the truth in them.

Suddenly a small girl ran across that immense salon, and tucked her hand in the marquis's own. She was hardly more than five or six years old, I judged, and I had to catch my breath at the beauty of this exquisite child as she looked shyly up at me and then at the marquis for assurance. Her rounded cheeks dimpled when she smiled at Jean.

"Aimée, *ma petite!*" Jean exclaimed as he reached down and scooped her up into his arms. Her gown of white muslin trimmed with satin ribbons was a miniature of my own lilac one, and her dark hair hung in a cloud of curls around her face.

The child laughed and hugged Jean. So this was the niece, I thought.

"Mademoiselle Tamar is the English lady your Uncle Jean rescued from the wicked pirates, Aimée," the marquis said indulgently. Then he glanced at me. "This is my grand-daughter, Tamar. As you can see, she has been told the story of the rescue already and has hardly been able to contain herself until she met the beautiful English mademoiselle."

She curtsied prettily for me, saying in a very mature voice, "*Bonjour*, Mademoiselle Tamar. Welcome to *le château*. I hope you will be very happy with us."

Moved deeply, strangely, I said, "*Merci*, Aimée. I see no reason why I should not be." And I knew that Neville did not know of her existence.

"Mademoiselle has promised to teach you some English, *ma petite*," Jean explained. I could see he delighted in this child. "Would you like a governess for a while?"

"*Mais oui!* I have never had a governess, have I, Uncle? *Maman* teaches me my lessons," she informed me.

"Well, you shall have one now, because you do need English," the marquis laughed. "Come along." He took the child's hand. "Let's take our mademoiselle to your *maman,* shall we? We've kept her waiting long enough."

My imaginings that Danielle was dead were completely wrong, for I knew at once that the woman sitting on the satin-covered chair was the woman in the locket, even though she was some-what older now. Her lustrous dark hair was coiled around her shapely head, and I thought the lovely eyes had a tragic expression in them, but perhaps I only imagined it.

"Danielle, may I have the pleasure of introduc-ing Jean's lovely fiancée, Mademoiselle Tamar Columb. Danielle is my eldest daughter, Tamar, and the mother of this charming little minx." He looked down at the little girl fondly. "And this gentleman behind her is Monsieur Michel Cot-tereau, my daughter's husband."

I was shocked: what I had built up in my mind did not include this. The man behind the chair was not at all like the Nicolas Cottereau I'd met last night: this man was much older, thick-set with broad shoulders, and rather stonefaced. He was not tall, yet large, and seemed short in comparison to both Jean and the marquis. Certainly he was not aristocratic. The thick dark hair was streaked with gray and he seemed out of place in this *grande salle*.

There could not have been a greater contrast ei-ther to the woman who was his wife. In her simple gown of wine-colored muslin with cream lace around the neckline and cuffs, she could not conceal her high-born beauty and elegance. She stood up and moved toward me with the grace and dignity of a queen.

"Welcome to Rouvroy, Tamar," she said in En-glish. "I am happy for both of you. When Jean told us about your daring escapade, it made us all marvel that you both escaped and are alive and well." She took me in her arms and kissed me on both cheeks. A faint sweet perfume clung around her. "You are exceptionally pretty too. Jean is fortunate." It caused me to blush at my deception.

"Thank you, madame," I said.

"You must call me Danielle. We're to be sisters."

I hoped Jean was hurting somewhere inside that black heart of his, I thought furiously. "Very well then. Danielle."

Satisfied, she looked to her husband. Michel Cottereau was less cordial, but I believed that was because he was at a disadvantage, for he did not speak English. I tried to recall what Jean had said about the Cottereau family, but I could not. His big hand covered mine, accepting me on the same terms as his wife had, and wished me well.

I glanced at Jean and fancied I saw great restraint between these two men. I believed Jean resented Michel for marrying his sister, and certainly he'd led me to believe the worst had happened to Danielle, although I could see nothing so tragic. But if she had suffered, was it not over now and best forgotten?

Danielle was saying, "I find it delightful that you allowed Jean to persuade you to come here, Tamar. And I am pleased you will be able to start Aimée on badly needed English lessons, for I have neglected this part of her education. Even Charette could use some lessons. I fear she would resent it, however."

So Jean persuaded me to come here, I thought with malice, and laughed. "I shall make mistakes, for I know nothing of teaching children," I said slowly, doubting my ability. And certainly I did not wish to have anything to do with the little firebrand Charette! I wondered where she was this morning.

Danielle smiled a beautiful smile. "No one expects miracles, least of all with Aimée. What with my duties at the Farms, it is not easy to educate as I would like to. You will be a godsend, truly."

No one excused the absent Charette, but Danielle informed me that Maurice was an aide-de-camp for one of the generals in Bonaparte's campaign, and in Spain at the moment. "We are against it, but Maurice keeps reminding us too often that we did not lose our heads or our lands by accepting the new order. He would do nothing less than join forces with the first consul. Perhaps that is best after all." I thought she said this with more than wistfulness.

A butler passed around the glasses of champagne, and a toast was drunk to the happiness of Jean and myself. It was strange that as I took that toast and shared it with Jean and his family, I felt a very real part of them, as though I were actually what Jean wanted them to believe I was, his promised bride.

So I said after a little while, "Maurice is your cousin? Charette's brother?"

Danielle nodded. "And a very high-spirited young man, I might add. I fear his sister has some of that spirit too, for she would not join us."

"Charette is in love with Jean," I said matter-of-factly, and Danielle's eyes opened wide. "She greeted Jean . . . last night," I explained, smiling.

"Oh, you must forgive her if you can, Tamar. She is still a child in many ways, and very fond of Jean—fiercely so, I'm afraid. But once she accepts you as Jean's choice, then she will no doubt come to her senses. I'm sure you can understand."

"But of course," I agreed, although I was not so sure I did. And then I recalled it was all pretense anyway. What would this woman think and say if she knew the whole truth?

Jean was talking to Michel and the marquis about the affairs of the château and the Farms, which I understood were Michel's, and Michel said bluntly, "Did you see that nephew of mine, Jean, when you put into port last evening?" A moment of awkwardness followed, and I supposed he was speaking of Nicolas Cottereau. Michel was frowning, clearly ill at ease, and this disturbed me for some reason.

"No. Should I have?" How blatantly he spoke, lying to suit himself, I thought. I was conscious of the anxiety Danielle was showing as she listened to the men.

"It seems that the diligence coming out from Rennes was attacked last evening," the marquis answered drily. "There was an inquiry at the Farms this morning by the police. Quite a vast sum of money was taken, intended for the garrison at Brest."

Jean crossed his arms over his chest, denial in his expression. "So you think it was Nicolas, Michel. But why? Unless—" He stopped. I would see his disapproval of this man, but I couldn't understand why.

The marquis lowered his voice and informed us, "It is just possible that the *Chouans* have taken the roads here again, and there will be a house-to-house inquiry. Naturally the police have not forgotten Michel's role in the past. Nicolas has not been here, for you may recall he was in exile, but rumors are that he has been seen. Of course those are only rumors, and certainly not facts. I suggest it was a case of robbery by the bandits we know that roam Brittany. Nothing more."

"And let's pray that is all it is, Monsieur le Marquis," Michel said dourly. "To have Nicolas here is dangerous. He is a troublemaker, that one, and he won't rest until he stirs up a hornet's nest among the citizens." He spoke harshly, and I couldn't help but recall to mind the man I'd met last night in that blue twilight within the trees.

Nor could I forget just how Jean and Nicolas had greeted each other. Hadn't Jean implied that he too was ready to take up arms against Bonaparte? And what of this Marquis de Rouvroy? Was he so entirely innocent, a "returned and forgiven ex-patriot" of Bourbon France? The unrest inside me brought a dim recollection of what Neville had said: "The War Department may have need of me in the near future, Tamar. That peace treaty is a breather, they think." And I wondered if he had suspected an uprising here in Brittany, and if the War Department would use him again as an agent. . . .

"We'll just have to deny it all when the police do come inquiring. I suppose it is that Labbé, poking his nose into every *affaire*?" Jean complained. "Don't tell me that he is in charge of the inquiries?" He lifted his brows menacingly.

The marquis nodded briefly, inclining his head. "He has a long memory. We watch what we do here these days, do we not, Michel? Bonaparte has a noose around our necks, or so we are led to believe." But I fancied I saw a gleam of humor behind those fine dark eyes as he looked at Jean.

Michel said nothing, but he scowled discontentedly, and Jean said, "I have promised to take Tamar on a tour of the château. I'm sure this talk of bandits and robberies and the problems of our New Republic is too much for her right now."

"Of course. How uncivil we must seem, after all she's been through," Danielle hurried to say. She touched my arm. "We shall have much to learn of each other, Tamar. Do not worry yourself on setting up lessons with Aimée until you've had a chance to settle in." She smiled. "Jean is an expert guide; you will learn your way around in no time."

The marquis stood beside her, a look of conspiracy on his face. It was then that I knew he knew everything, and I went almost weak from this truth. I was sure that Jean had taken him into his confidence.

It was one of those days that comes at the end of September on the coast in Brittany as well as Cornwall. Gold sunlight reflected on the stone walls of the château so that the stones shimmered gold and silver, and vivid colors of the flowers in the gardens stood out, and I was aware of late summer red roses crawling over crenellated walls, and ivy already touched with scarlet stretching across stones to distant towers. Such days had existed in Cornwall. . . .

I was also conscious of Jean's hand on my arm as he led me around the house, and the strange tingle it caused beneath the muslin alarmed me. I resented what his nearness aroused within me, and I fought it constantly.

"You are acting out your role with the convincing art of a true actress, mademoiselle. I must congratulate you, for it seems I miscalculated." I caught my breath sharply, turning to him, pulling my arm free.

"Miscalculated? Monsieur, that seems to be your . . . your great problem in life!" I was angry. I knew my eyes flashed at him, my color high with emotion. "The marquis, your uncle, if indeed he is your uncle, *knows*, doesn't he? He knows *everything*."

"My dear Mademoiselle Tamar!" he exclaimed, feigning surprise. "You shock me. You are upset." His lifted eyebrows made me think of a satyr.

"It's all a ploy, isn't it? You said your uncle told you the story; you said he knew my brother, so that means he knows who I am. You both planned to abduct me; you planned it so my brother would come after me. You even lied about seeing Nicolas Cottereau last night." I was blind with fury against this man.

He shrugged. "What Michel doesn't know about Nicolas and his work is surely best under any circumstances."

I went on. "Danielle. I see it all clearly now. You led me to believe some great tragedy had taken her life. Implied, no, *accused* my brother of being the cause of that tragedy, even going so far as to make me believe that her child was my brother's, while in truth Monsieur Michel Cottereau—"

"You mistake me, mademoiselle!" His voice cut like a whip across my own, and his fingers gripped my wrists like bands of steel. He brought me face to face with him, and the anger I saw there astounded me. "Aimée is not Michel Cottereau's daughter! Never! My sister and Michel have been married only these past six months. Aimée's father is an Englishman. Aimée's father is Neville Columb."

My wrists hurt from his grip and I said, "You're hurting me, monsieur." He suddenly released me. I was angry, but something rose up like a well of water inside me, and it was all I could do to keep my tears back. I swallowed hard. "Why do you not leave the past alone? Your sister has a future with her new husband. What does it matter now, even to you, who the child's father is? Why make your sister suffer by bringing my brother here, if what you say is true?"

"Your brother must know the price my sister paid after he abandoned her!" He seemed shaken by a violence smoldering in him perhaps for years. "It is a debt of honor that he must be made to pay. I have sworn I will not rest until I find the man who hurt Danielle and betrayed my parents. That is something I owe them, to find this man who brought them to their deaths."

"What then, monsieur? Danielle will suffer all over again, will she not? And Michel is her husband now. What chance of happiness will she have with him, if she is forced to relive her painful past?"

"She should not have married Michel—"

"But she must have . . . needed Michel to have

married him. Surely you cannot begrudge her what happiness she can find with him?"

He looked at me strangely, darkly, as if he were seeing me for the first time.

"Danielle is not happy, as you may discover in time." His voice was heavy with sadness, and I dared not speak lest he hear in my voice that very same sorrow.

We were enemies; but his family had accepted me unaware of the true circumstances and I wondered what they would do when the time came for that truth to be uncovered. Jean had taken it upon himself to even old scores that should have been left in that tragic past.

But what were his intentions? To have Neville return to the scene of the tragedy? What did he hope to gain?

A bevy of mixed emotions waged a battle deep inside me. "You seem to believe there will be time for this . . . discovery, monsieur," I found myself saying.

Devilish laughter stirred in those eyes now as I glanced up, finding them on my face. "Oh, I'm sure you will discover many things in the time you are here, Mademoiselle Tamar. In a château this size—"

"Jean! Jean!" A voice broke in on us as we were passing through a large courtyard, and we both turned to see Charette running toward us, her blue riding habit showing off her lovely figure. A riding crop in her gloved hands, she hurried up to Jean and smiled up at him coquettishly.

"I've been hoping you would be free. I did not want to join such a boring hour with the family, and I've been waiting for you. I have the mounts ready. We can ride out to our castle." She ignored me completely, and it did not go unnoticed by Jean.

"Charette. Aren't you forgetting your manners? Mademoiselle Tamar will think you are rude." If his words were hard, his voice was not, but the effect was as if he'd slapped her.

She stepped back, her eyes wide. She put one hand up to her mouth, and stared at me.

I put out my hand, but she ignored it, her eyes on my face, then on Jean's. "No! No! I won't speak to her! I won't have anything to do with her! You can't . . . marry . . . *her!*" She turned and ran, disappearing through one of the arches.

I met Jean's glance coolly. "Hadn't you best go after her, perhaps . . . explain?" In a strange way I thought he was being unnecessarily cruel to this young girl who was so much in love with him.

"Explain? My dear Miss Tamar, Charette needs to be brought down to earth. She fancies she is in love with me, but I can assure you it is a child's love."

"You need not put yourself out to assure me, monsieur!" I exclaimed. "You had best try to assure *her* of your intentions!"

"Oh, but I will do that, and now, *ma chère* Tamar!" And before I could protest, he moved, and I was in his arms, his mouth on mine. One hand moved up behind my head, and I was aware of a disturbing sensation so demanding that it consumed every thought. I forgot the courtyard we were standing in, the gaping servants, and I even forgot that I abhorred this Frenchman, my enemy. I closed my eyes and melted in his arms.

When he lifted his face from mine, I opened my eyes and knew I was a completely different person. He was staring down into my eyes, seeing everything. I don't know how long that moment was, but it seemed as if a century passed before I emerged from the haze of desire.

He stood back, yet still held me; then something changed in his face, a wicked look clouded his eyes. I blinked, my face burning under his scrutiny. Then I followed Jean's gaze out toward the garden where Charette stood watching, her face twisted with jealousy. When she saw us looking at her, she darted from our sight again.

Jean was silent for a moment, then said quietly, "It is all right, *ma chère*. I had to show her—" He had used me, ruthlessly, to break his cousin's heart. He had seen into my own heart, and had known what was there.

"You must believe me, Tamar. Charette is too possessive. It is best that she learn now."

"So you used me to teach that broken-hearted girl how brutal a man like you can be!" I could hardly keep my voice from trembling. It was no little matter, and I was stunned when his words echoed my thoughts.

"I know it is no small matter to a young girl like Charette. Deep inside her she is warm and generous and one day she will fall in love with the right man. Right now, she has this obsession, and it must not be allowed to ruin her."

Much later I was to recall his words and how he'd spoken them—not unkindly, but as someone who really loved her deeply for what she was to him. But then I could not see beyond my own fury; I knew now that it was because my heart had betrayed me, and I believed he'd wanted to humiliate me.

"You are a cruel teacher, then, monsieur, playing with hearts at your own whim. She is crushed because of your well-meaning lesson. I think she may not forget so easily—" and I was on the verge of saying, "and neither will I," but I checked my tongue in time, blushing hotly.

"You are angry with me, my dear Tamar," he said lightly, still holding my arm as though he expected me to run away from him as Charette had. When I didn't answer, he went on, "Now I think I had better show you our dungeons before you do have a chance to change your mind about me. These dungeons may make an everlasting impression upon you."

"Barbarian!" I cried, meeting his eyes, only to have him throw back his head and laugh out loud.

"Then come. I will show you the barbarian's dungeon." He was amused.

He took my arm and led me across the courtyard and through a stone arch into what was the ground floor chamber of the nearest tower. We went through a door and down a rather long corridor with only narrow slits for light to come through. It smelled dank and musty, and when at last we came to an iron door, Jean drew back the heavy bolts and lifted the latch. It swung open. Instantly the wind rushed in from the sea so that I was blown back, and Jean steadied me with his arm about my waist.

"Careful here," he said. "Hold on to me, for it's slippery here." And he brought me close to the edge. I stared down at the rocks, green with slime and seaweed, and then at the churning ocean below.

"Sometimes when the tide is exceptionally high the water comes up to those iron manacles you see down there." He pointed down to the round iron rings attached to the walls and crusted over with rust and age and sea salt. "And then the prisoners drown," he said without emotion.

Horrified, I stepped back, only to have his hands hold me fast. I turned my face away, and he pulled me back through the door, then closed it and bolted it.

"I can see that you are not too impressed with our methods of subduing the enemy, Tamar. I suggest we curtail our tour of the real dungeons, and instead go through a portion of the château. It is, as you have seen, a vast house, and it will take a while to see it all."

As we toured the lovely château, I found myself actually forgetting the awful situation that had brought me there. I was amazed at the vast beauty of the place, and despite the lack of servants to keep it from falling into disrepair, it was still a magnificent house.

"We were fortunate, that is about all," Jean explained, "not to have had it razed during the peasants' revolt at the outbreak of the Revolution. My parents were gone, of course, and when the peasants came, only the influence of the Cottereau family kept the château safe from the vandals and brigands who came out of Paris when the prisons were broken into and the innocents were slaughtered *en masse.*"

I tried to picture it; I'd heard about it, and I knew my brother had played some part in that tragic time. "Your parents had returned by that time?" I found myself asking.

He nodded. "Yes. Before that actually. They came back with Danielle. I was furious because they allowed her to join the Royalist cause, and would not allow me to do so. But it was the Cottereau family that saved the château."

I was quiet, thinking of that time and how it must have caused his parents much anxiety to have to depend on someone else to save their property. "The Cottereau family, then," I said, "must have been very close to your own. I mean, it could not have been an easy task to protect the château, yet they did it."

Jean could not hide his feelings.

"They are a very proud family, and as old as the Rouvroy family here in Brittany. My father and Nicolas's father were good friends and felt the same way about France. I believe they made a pact between them, although I do not really know what kind of pact it was. And they fought side by side, through it all, and died for the cause they believed in."

I tried to picture it. It was not easy, but it never is when one has never known such a thing. We were silent for a while, and then I said, "I understood that Michel Cottereau was part of that cause. Was he not joined with his brother in all of it? Would he not have known your parents in those times?"

He turned to face me. "No. Michel does not know who they were. I believe he suspected, but he did not know, for it was a well-kept secret. I am sure it was only Nicolas's father who knew their true identities." That contempt I'd heard earlier when he spoke of Michel was in his voice again.

"You are bitter toward Michel, aren't you?"

He was not smiling. "Very much so, I fear."

"Because he married your sister? But surely—" I didn't understand, and I knew he saw my puzzlement.

"Danielle married to save the family honor, that is all. He was after her long ago, when she was a beautiful young girl. I remember how he used to watch her, anytime—out riding, or when she left the house to step into the carriage, whenever he could. The possessive look he always wore made me want to strike him across the face, but I was consoled by the fact that she would have nothing to do with Michel then. She often went to Versailles with our parents, and sometimes I went too. She could have had any man she chose."

"You care for her very deeply," I said, understanding.

He nodded, and when he didn't pursue it, I asked, "She knows, then, that your parents are dead, and how they died?"

"Yes. It was a very hard time for her too, and that is why, after all her . . . suffering, that she should give herself to Michel brings a bitter taste to my mouth. He hardly recognizes Aimée, and

I'm sure he thinks of the child as the bastard of an unknown lover. He is fiercely jealous."

"You do not regard your niece as such?" I knew I had touched a vulnerable spot, for a dark flush appeared on his face.

"Aimée is an innocent victim, and she is Danielle's daughter. I accept her as she is, a lovable, innocent girl in much need of affection."

He led me down a corridor that I recognized as the one where my rooms were, and when we came to the door he opened it, holding it for me to pass through. It was a gesture that said his little act of being my lover was over for this hour. I had the absurd feeling of wanting to laugh, but all I could manage was to give him a cool mocking stare, reminding him that I had not forgotten I was here under duress.

It was a chilly parting, and I was glad to be alone, for I was more than disturbed about my own emotions. Never in my life had I known such mixed feelings, and for the first time someone had stepped between me and my brother.

I was restless; I went to stand at the window of the boudoir, and flung the casement wide open. Leaning there, I was glad of the fresh air on my face. The scent of flowers stole up from the gardens and I could hear the strange little click of the cicadas. I was so absorbed in my thoughts that when I heard the faint sound of voices below me, I barely noticed at all—until I heard Jean's voice and I had to listen.

"Jean, was it Nicolas you saw last night?" It was Danielle who asked the question.

"Yes. Of course it was."

"What does it all mean, Jean? Is it all starting over again? I couldn't bear—"

"Don't worry, Danielle. You won't be involved anymore. I'll see to that. But we can't ignore what is to come."

"It is dangerous. The whole of the coast is being watched. You took a chance."

"I know. But we were cautious, and we shall continue to be so. Believe me."

They were directly below me, and I suppose I should have moved back into the room. But I guessed they would have difficulty seeing me, so I stayed where I was.

Danielle said, "You should not have brought the English girl here, Jean. You know how Monsieur Labbé is. He will not rest until he learns all—"

"She is safe enough, Danielle. You must be kind to her."

"Of course. Of course." There was a silence, then Danielle spoke softly. "Charette is being very difficult, Jean. We can do nothing with her, I fear."

"I know. I had no idea she was so set on—"

"Well, yes. We all knew she was bound up in this fascination for you. When Maurice was here last, he warned her, but she would not listen."

"She will have to learn differently, Danielle. You know that," Jean answered angrily.

"Oh, yes, of course I do. So you care for this English girl, Jean? What a different name! Tamar Columb. Unusual, and she is very charming and pretty. But I'm afraid you'll have to explain it all to Charette."

"I have tried to make her understand Danielle . . ."

I moved away, my face burning, my heart trembling. Jean had done well in deceiving his sister.

4

All of what Jean had told me stayed heavily on my mind throughout the rest of the day. I found I could think of nothing else.

Neville. Danielle. Aimée. What had seemed so preposterously impossible, so absurd that I had not considered it for one moment, was now staring me in the face, and I knew I had to come to terms with it.

There was the locket, and no matter how I tried to shrug it off, I knew that because I had found it at Columb Manor, it was the tangible link which brought me to reconsider Jean's accusations. Yet I could not accept that my own brother was capable of that betrayal; it went against all of what I knew of his character.

But just how well did I know my brother? His life had been locked up from me, and he'd shown only what he'd wanted me to see. I found myself totally bewildered and quite helpless.

When I went down for the midday meal, I could not keep myself from searching Aimée's face as she laughed or mimicked her mother or her Uncle Jean. I probed for resemblances, however slight, to Neville; but of course there were none, even in her eyes, for the color there was more like my own than that of Neville's.

It was Danielle who unwittingly tallied the score for me, plunging me into grief for weeks to come. Jean had disappeared after that meal with a sullen Charette, and Danielle asked me if I would walk with her to the convent where Aimée took her lessons in needlework.

It was a perfect afternoon. We left the château through the gardens, walking down a winding path through an apple orchard, with Aimée dancing delightedly in front of us, her little bonnet tied with pale lavender ribbons bobbing up and down as she skipped along.

"You can't possibly know what it was like here, Tamar, when the church was taken from us. One good thing Bonaparte has done for us is that he gave us back our religion after all those years having been denied it."

"How do you mean?"

"Everyone's life, the peasants' especially so, was centered around the church, and at the Revolution all the clergy were turned out, even hunted down in some cases, and the churches used as barns, stables, or worse. It was not a good time—no. Our own convent was rendered helpless, of course, and the good sisters were scattered like lost sheep and kept in hiding; but now they have returned and are very poor. So you see, they can use students like my Aimée, even though they don't allow me to pay them very much."

"It must have been hard," I said with quick sympathy. "The old way must have been very hard to give up."

She glanced at me and I saw a flash of fire in her dark eyes. I guessed that behind that quiet exterior there lived great passion and pride. But she dismissed it with a gesture.

"It is gone, the old way. I suppose Jean has told you some of the humiliations our people had to suffer?"

"Yes. He has told me some of it."

She sighed. "I don't care who rules in Paris now, except that it would bring peace to our land. Too many of us have died. It will take a long time to forget that." I knew she was speaking of her parents, and perhaps was referring to her own role in the war.

Tall hollyhock bordered the orchard path we walked through. The scent of fruit still on the trees was heavy like wine itself, and soon we came to the convent, a small group of stone buildings clustered around a courtyard. Danielle rang the bell, and we waited by the door. When it opened, a small woman in black and white habit smiled, greeting us warmly.

"Sister Magdaleine, please meet Mademoiselle Columb from England," Danielle said in French. "She is my brother's fiancée."

"*Bonjour,* mademoiselle. Welcome to our convent."

I thanked her politely, knowing that one day there would be a dreadful reckoning for all the lies that Jean was sowing. But for now it almost seemed real, and as Aimée handed Sister Magdaleine the little bunch of marigolds she had picked along the path, the nun invited both Danielle and me to have a glass of apple wine in the garden while we waited for Aimée's class to finish.

Sitting there with Danielle, I wanted to ask her a thousand questions, but I did not know where to start. If she had known her English lover's real name, she would have recognized my own last name. Could it be that Neville would not have told her if he had been the Englishman? When Danielle next spoke, it almost stunned me.

"You have a most unusual name, Tamar."

"It's Cornish," I said proudly, if a bit shakily. "The River Tamar divides the rest of England on the Devon side, cutting it off from the Duchy of Cornwall. I'm named after this river, but our manor is near Falmouth, farther south and on the coast. My home is quite like Brittany, I think." Thinking of Columb Manor almost brought tears to my eyes, and I averted my face so that Danielle could not see the longing I felt.

Danielle was saying, ". . . someone once told me of that Duchy of Cornwall, crossing the River at Saltash in a place he said was called Plymouth. He said it was a different world to go into the duchy—those were his very words, I recall. He also compared it to Brittany and our coast here. . . ." Her voice faded, and I glanced at her sharply, aware that she had suddenly slipped back into that private time only she knew, and my heart thudded inside me.

So it was true, I thought, swallowing hard. She

was speaking of Neville. I did not pursue it; I did not want to know any more. It was as if all those pieces of a puzzle were now being placed together to make a picture I never knew existed, and somehow I did not want to look at it, not now.

Danielle suddenly was conscious of how I'd looked at her and I know she felt the strain between us, so I turned away again as she said, "You must forgive me, my dear, for going on so. There are so many things in one's life that one should forget, or try to . . ." She left off, and because I felt so guilty, I found myself saying the words I hadn't planned to say.

"He must have been . . . special to you." I met her eyes, and they revealed everything. "I mean, for you to remember."

She glanced away from me to the small cup of wine. "He was Aimée's father," she said simply, unashamed.

My mouth was dry. I wanted to ask her more questions, but the words would not come out, and I stood up, walking over to the low wall that separated the garden from a small olive grove. "It must be painful for you, then, to speak of it."

She inclined her head to one side, and stood up to walk over beside me, her face a mask of serenity now. "No. Not anymore. That time is gone. Aimée is six years old now, and I must see that she is happy."

"You are married to Michel Cottereau. He is a good father to her, is he not?" I searched her face, but she successfully hid any unhappiness that Jean had imagined, I thought.

She merely nodded. "They are not close, and

perhaps never will be, but then, she will not suffer under him. He is a kind man, if not affectionate."

"You have not been married long, then?"

"Six months," she said.

"Do you live at the Farms, or in the château? I understand Michel runs the Farms."

"We have an apartment in the château, for Father likes me to run the place for him. But Michel often stays at the Farms. It creates less problems this way."

At that moment, Charette appeared through the small gate in the high stone wall, looking very pleased with herself and certainly she was a vision of beauty in the soft russet gown she was wearing. Danielle was as surprised to see her as I was.

"There you are," Charette offered, smiling coquettishly. "I was sent to inform you, and to fetch you if necessary, Danielle dear. We have visitors, and Uncle Honoré requests that you hurry back with me." Her words were sugary sweet as her eyes slid over me and rested back on her cousin's face.

"Oh, dear!" She bit her lip. "I suppose Sister Magdaleine could bring Aimée back to the château . . ." She hesitated.

"Her governess could do it so easily, Danielle, I'm sure. Is that not one of your duties? She wouldn't mind looking after her charge," Charette said, ignoring me still. I was uneasy, and wondered what Jean could have said to her to give her that cunning, smug look. But thankfully Danielle came to my defense.

"You should be more considerate of Jean's fiancée, Charette. She is not a governess in that sense. You must apologize at once."

Charette flushed at the rebuke. "You take offense too quickly, Cousin Danielle. I understood mademoiselle was to act as governess to Aimée. That is all."

"It is not like that, Charette my dear. Above all, Tamar is Jean's chosen bride-to-be." She spoke kindly yet firmly.

"Is she? I wonder. I wonder if she is what she says she is?" A shy smile curved her pink lips, and for a moment I was speechless, as was Danielle.

"This is really too much, Charette. Apologies at once, or you shall indeed—"

"Oh, for heaven's sake, Danielle. If it means that much to you! But I really can't see that it would harm . . . mademoiselle . . . if she stayed here and then brought Aimée back with her. We haven't all day, and your father, the marquis—"

"Charette!" Danielle flashed at her. "You are being very rude and childish. I insist that you apologize to Tamar right now."

The girl seemed to hesitate and, a little fearful, she turned to me. She mumbled, "I am . . . sorry." That was all.

But I said, "Thank you, Charette. You know, I think I should like this chance to get to know Aimée, and I should truly like to wait for her. Please do not think it remiss if you need to hurry back to the château."

"Very well, my dear. You know the way back, and Aimée is familiar with the path. I shan't worry then." She leaned over and kissed my cheek, that scent of sweet perfume about her. "How good you are to look after my daughter. She will be happy that you wanted to walk her home."

"It will be a pleasure, I assure you, Danielle."

She smiled. "Come then, Charette. Let us be off. Surely the visitor must be very important for my father to have me attend. Do you know who is calling, Charette?"

The girl shrugged. "It is the chief of police, Monsieur Labbé. It was he who wanted to talk with you, Danielle."

I saw the shock in Danielle's eyes, while at the same time there was a certain malice and insolence in the girl's manner.

"With me? But why?"

"How should I know? Perhaps he has found something that will help to learn the truth of that stolen gold from the diligence last evening. I also heard a rumor about a shipment of arms and ammunition brought over from England. And the Château de Rouvroy is not above suspicion." There was a curious look of triumph in those black eyes.

"What could any of that have to do with us?" Danielle asked.

"I'm sure you would know the answer to that better than I." Charette shrugged her shoulders. "You played a part in the Resistance, and therefore you come under suspicion—Monsieur Labbé's suspicion. Maurice always said that anyone who was on the other side during the revolt would be under the first consul's suspicion."

Danielle was silent to this, and I couldn't help but think that she wanted to shake the girl for speaking as she did. There was a tiny smile on

Charette's face, almost as if she were amused by Danielle's concern.

"Forgive me, Tamar, but I see I must not keep Monsieur Labbé waiting. He just may decide to lock me up again. That man brings back terrible memories I can't tear from my mind! The very fact that he is here at the château makes me afraid."

"But it is so long past," I said, yet I knew that past was emerging again to haunt her.

"The past to Monsieur Labbé is a huge sore that has festered for years, and he won't be satisfied until he has his revenge." Her voice held all the contempt she had for this man, along with the bitterness of a woman who's suffered too much. I wanted to learn more, but Charette was already walking through the garden toward the gate in the wall. Danielle touched my arm briefly before following her.

"Jean will have something to say, I know, and I must not keep them waiting. I will tell him where you are." Smiling again, she turned and followed Charette.

I had nearly half an hour to wait, so I turned and strolled through the small well-kept garden. Marigolds and dahlias bloomed here; there was an herbaceous border where I recognized fennel, coriander, and tarragon among other plants, and a waft of spiciness touched my nostrils, pungent and sweet.

This garden was adjacent to the olive grove, but separated from it by a low stone wall. I went through the gate and stepped into the grove where long yellowed grasses grew thick and where the heavy mesh nets had been laid out to catch the dark olives under the trees.

I was trying to sort out my thoughts as I stood beside an ancient gray-black tree, when I became aware of two people standing near the wall ahead of me. They did not see me, I was sure, and their voices were so low I could not distinguish them; but after a moment I saw that it was a sister from the convent speaking with a tall man in brown hunting leather. She left him suddenly, and retreated back through a door into the wall of the convent.

I would not have given it another thought, except the man turned and saw me immediately. He laughed, as recognition came into his expression. The man I knew as Nicolas Cottereau strolled over to me, surprise in his bold eyes as I was sure it was in mine.

"Mademoiselle Columb, *n'est-ce pas?*" He smiled provocatively, and I had to admit he was attractive in a swashbuckling manner, younger than I'd believed him to be.

"*Bonjour,* Monsieur Cottereau," I said, wondering why he might be at the convent.

"How are you getting on at the château, mademoiselle? Was not the marquis surprised to find that you are engaged to Jean, eh? When is the betrothal going to be announced? I suspect the fiery little Charette will sting like a scorpion now that you have come along and snatched her man from her!" He laughed and I despised him for this.

"How do you know this?" I could not help saying.

He lifted his eyebrows. "I know Charette, mademoiselle."

I could not understand how he could know so much about her if he'd been in exile, as everyone had led me to believe. But I did not intend to stop and gossip with this man whose eyes seemed never to miss a thing. He seemed too familiar, and it gave me a feeling of unease.

So I said rather bluntly, "Was it you, monsieur, who robbed the diligence from Rennes last evening?" I saw the quick flash in his eyes, the stillness of his body before he spoke. "So you know about that, mademoiselle?" He shrugged. "It shouldn't surprise me that you would know it. But I can promise you one thing, Miss Tamar. And that is that it went to a good cause."

"What cause?"

"Your brother's cause, Miss Tamar. And our cause as well."

I stood there aghast for an instant. I could not move or speak, and I felt myself go pale as death. "What—what are you talking about?" I managed to ask. "How do you know my brother?"

"That would be telling, wouldn't it?" He flashed a smile, the teeth as white as I remembered them. "But the less we know of each other, the better off we'll be, agreed? I know you won't run to the police, for that would involve you all the more. Let's forget this encounter, Miss Tamar."

I remembered suddenly why Charette had come to fetch Danielle to the château. Without thinking, I said, "The police are at the château right now, it seems. Making inquiries of that robbery last night." I could have bitten off my tongue for informing him of that. I thought he seemed surprised, but he only shrugged.

"You don't say! Then it is best if you know even less of me, mademoiselle. You have not seen me here, *n'est-ce pas?*" And before I could protest, he reached out and took my hand, gallantly brushing it with his lips.

"*Au revoir.*" He moved swiftly into the trees and out of sight.

I scarcely knew I had walked back through the gate; my hand trembled on the latch, my thoughts churning over and over. He knew my brother. He knew then that Jean had been to England. Hadn't he waited on the shore for him? The *cause*—he'd said it was my brother's cause—and that could only mean one thing: he knew Neville was coming back to France as an agent. A spy.

It was obvious, all of it. Jean's going to England, the robbery, the appearance of Nicolas, the inquiry of the police chief . . . Nicolas and Jean and the marquis had probably even planned my abduction as a ruse to bring Neville to Brittany. I knew Danielle's plight was not the only reason for Jean bringing me here. I *knew* it.

My heart gave a great jolt. Neville. Hadn't he said the War Department needed his services again? But he had also said he'd refused them point blank for the time being. That meant he had not wished to leave England, so Jean and Nicolas had to scheme to get him back into the role of *chevalier* for the cause. The cause—the remaking of a vital stand for the Bourbons with the backing of English gold, arms, and ammunition.

Jean had spoken of the *Chouans* with fervent

pride; he had evaded a direct answer to my question of taking up arms against Bonaparte, but now I was convinced that Jean was leading the *Chouan* movement with Nicolas. He'd used his own ship while Nicolas waited on shore, and Nicolas had robbed the diligence of its gold.

Thinking of Neville brought to mind Cameron Pennland; I closed my eyes and tried to put his face before me, but it was Jean de Rouvroy's face that appeared. Disturbed, I opened my eyes and thought I might still be dreaming when I saw Jean walking toward me through the garden gate.

Just to see him brought such intense pleasure, mingled with my dislike of him, that I was angry with myself. As he walked over and came to my side, I tried to keep my composure, but his eyes were intent on my face, making me uneasy.

"I must speak with you, Tamar." His voice was just above a whisper.

"Very well," I said, waiting. But he gestured toward the olive grove, and I couldn't help thinking that Nicolas had been here only moments before, secretly meeting one of the sisters in the convent.

Not until we were a short distance from the walls of the convent did Jean stop and turn to face me. In the shadowy light I saw a deep frown on his face.

"I thought it would be safe if I brought you here," he said, "but it looks as if I am wrong. Will you forgive me, Tamar?"

My heart gave a queer little lurch. "Why? What has happened to make you change your mind?"

He was quiet a long moment before speaking.

"The chief of police came to the château making inquiries, and it upset Danielle greatly. It brought back all the old painful memories to her. Fortunately I was there to put Labbé in his place."

"Does he suspect you are involved with last night's . . . affair?"

"You do not know Monsieur Labbé, Tamar. He is a man who would suspect his own mother. I must not allow him to frighten Danielle again. She has suffered so much. I can't allow it to go on."

I was silent at this, and a moment later I asked, "What has this to do with my being here?"

He was close to me, his nearness warm, and I felt a tingle the moment his eyes touched mine. "It was madness, sheer madness, that led me to bring you here, taking you as I did from your home. I should not have listened to Uncle Henri and his wild scheme to force your brother to come to our cause. *Mon Dieu,* I wanted revenge on the man who deserted my sister, but now . . ." He stopped, looking at me.

"But now?"

"I was desperate to get even with your brother, to make him suffer. Believe me, Tamar, I did not want to harm you. That is why I made up the lie about your being my fiancée. It seemed safe, and it is so, as you are under my protection. But already Monsieur Labbé knows about your presence here. And that you are English."

"Surely we are not at war with France, and there are many English in this country. So why should he be suspicious? Does he not know the

. . . tale of the daring rescue from the Barbary pirates?" I lifted my brows and smiled.

"Yes, he was informed of that, and made a statement that he would want to meet the *demoiselle* Jean de Rouvroy rescued and is engaged to marry." He spoke with the same contempt I heard in Danielle's voice.

"But he suspects me nevertheless? Is that what you are trying to say?"

"You must not be frightened. He cannot do anything. I will not let him question you."

"You are afraid that I might reveal what I know?"

"You would be right in doing so; I couldn't blame you if you did. But that would only jeopardize your brother, and involve you at once. I feel so guilty now. I wanted you to know."

He stretched out his hand and turned my face toward him. "I . . . care, Tamar. I care what happens to you. Will you believe that?"

A thrill ran through me. "Yes."

"I am crazy to think it, but, *mon Dieu,* is it just possible that we are both struck with this madness?"

"Yes," I whispered. He leaned forward and kissed me gently on the lips. It was different from his kisses earlier, but still demanding. We were quite still for a moment, just staring at one another, so close there was no need for words. I stood back, marveling at the change in us.

"Why don't you despise me, Tamar?" There was an urgent note in his voice.

"That's a silly question now," I said in a hushed, tight voice.

"No. It's important that I know. I must know."

"I *should* despise you. But can't you guess?" We were so close, so achingly close that I could feel the pulsebeat between us.

His grip tightened, and he pulled me to him. His kisses were not gentle now. They were fierce and demanding, and I wanted them passionately. When at last I was able to step back, I said rather shakily, "What will Charette say?"

He jerked away. "What has Charette to do with this?"

"Everything it seems. She loves you."

He made a violent gesture. "She doesn't know what she feels. I'm her cousin."

"Have you spoken to her about it?"

"I don't have to. She knows. And that is why I am glad you are here, Tamar. She will have to accept you for what you are to me."

"And that is . . . ?" I probed, insistent but unsure.

"You are my fiancée."

"It is a pretense," I said quietly.

"Not after this," he said, and brought his arms around me, pulling me to him. The complete wonder of it all was that I had to believe him. His kisses were sweet and I didn't want him to stop.

It was he who put me from him. He was serious when he said, "Tamar, listen to me. You must not be afraid. I know we are involved in something very serious and very dangerous."

"It concerns my brother too," I said. "You want him here to help in the cause?"

He nodded. "Yes. He knows all the tactics. My uncle vows there is not another agent so clever and cunning as was Marc Renoire. We need him."

"You went to England to pick up arms and ammunition, as well as to convince my brother of this need of his special services?"

He took my hand, holding it for a moment before he kissed it. "You are clever, my dear Tamar. You could be a spy also." His smile was teasing. "How did you learn this?"

"It was something Charette said, a rumor of sorts, that a shipment had come from England. Then Nicolas practically convinced me it was true."

I felt him go still. "Nicolas? Where in God's name did you see him? When?"

"Not more than thirty minutes ago, right here in this olive grove."

"What was he doing here?"

I shrugged. "I have no idea. But he saw me, too, after the sister left him and went back into the convent."

"What did Nicolas say to you?" I thought he seemed anxious, disquieted somehow.

"Jean, he knows who I am, and he knows my brother. He was in on the plot, was he not, from the beginning?"

He hesitated, then said, "Yes. He was with me, in fact. Not at Columb Manor, but before I went to Cornwall. He returned a fortnight ago, I believe."

Something clicked in my mind. "Did he—did he go there, to London, I mean, to see my brother?"

Jean was not looking at me. But he said, "I believe that was his purpose, as he had direct information from my uncle who had already contacted your War Department regarding the whereabouts of one Marc Renoire. I suppose he felt Nicolas could persuade this one agent easily enough."

"But, in fact, he did not persuade him?" I asked.

He turned to look at me. "The method we used was our last resort, Tamar. We knew he would be forced to come if his sister were taken by force."

"You had your reasons. . . ."

"They were not good reasons. Will you forgive me?"

I thought about it. "Yes." I must be crazy, I thought, but I didn't care.

"You must not be frightened, Tamar. I am going to keep you out of all . . . this. And I won't let anyone hurt my sister as she was hurt before. She lived in perpetual fear for so long that I cannot allow the cause to cheat her of what she wants for Aimée. Can you understand that?"

A tiny voice within me said warningly, "If my brother comes here, how will she fare seeing him again? Or for that matter, how much will it cost my brother to be reminded of his past—of Danielle, and their child?"

But I said, "Yes, I can understand."

"Then will you help me, Tamar? I have so many forces fighting within me, and sometimes I do not have a clear sense of purpose. Trust me. Try to trust me." And I knew he was saying aloud the things that had been eating away at his conscience for years.

"I . . . I will trust you," I said with my heart,

but later I was to wonder if I had been too hasty.

Again he pressed my hand, kissing it, and said, "We had better fetch our little Aimée, or Danielle will wonder if she was right to leave you with her," and he laughed.

When we returned to the garden, Aimée was coming out of the convent, Sister Magdaleine behind her. When she saw Jean and me, she smiled and I could see she sensed the emotions between us. I was aware that my face was flushed with my happiness, but I didn't care.

Jean scooped Aimée up onto his shoulder, and then we bid the sister *bonjour,* and made our way back to the château.

When I came down to dinner that evening, I was aware of how I'd changed inside, looking at the whole world in a completely different light. To be in love, and for the first time, was like walking through a dense fog of rose-tinted clouds. It was sheer joy just to be near Jean and feel his eyes upon me from time to time. But it was with annoyance too that I found myself watching Charette's every glance and Jean's response to it, although now I knew there could be nothing between them.

She was so beautiful, her eyes bright and alive, and her deep orange muslin gown made my own white one seem drab. But I believe it was that night that she guessed the truth about Jean and me, and it prompted what followed afterward. They all should have seen it coming, for they knew her and I didn't. But it seemed that no one knew her very well after all.

The conversation through dinner centered on Labbé's unwelcome visit. Apparently Michel had not enjoyed knowing the police had been at the château. "Nosing around like a hound at bay," he said gruffly. "I honestly can't see why he would need to interrogate you, Danielle. You have nothing to do with that nephew of mine, do you?" He glanced at his wife who, though elegant in a deep violet silk gown with lace around the low neckline, seemed unduly distraught.

The marquis said, "Of course she doesn't, Michel. Why should she? But Labbé will play his little games with us all. We must be prepared for it." He said it with a trace of cynicism.

"Prepared?" remarked Michel. "You'd think we're all under some yoke of bondage the way Monsieur Labbé stalks about. I'd give anything to know what that nephew of mine is doing. I could understand it if he was intending to come back under the new system as a repatriot. But I suppose in due time I shall get a visit from him. And when I do, he'll get a piece of my mind."

"Come now, Michel," the marquis said. "You surely haven't forgotten the days when your own brothers were up in arms against the revolutionists. Nicolas must feel very much the same. . . ." He stopped, and I could feel the tension around us.

"But we were at war then, and we are *not* at war now," Michel said, "All that is dead, and if Nicolas doesn't have the sense to see that Bonaparte will get what he wants, then he is in for a lot of trouble."

"There are rumors that say the peace treaty is

only a stall for time," the marquis went on. "Bonaparte has made himself first consul, and it means he is trying to persuade us all that he can be made emperor. Imagine that! If that's the case, we'll be back at war before another year passes, for not one of us will stand for such audacity. Rather our Bourbon successor than him in Paris!"

Then Danielle said, "You speak as if the king's cause is still sacred. Too many died for that cause, may I remind you, and too many of us lived in fear because of it. There were none of us who did not tremble for our loved ones, and now you speak of war like it is God's own answer! I don't care what happens to that fat old Bourbon who ran like a coward to England, not once risking *his* life! I only care for those who are dear to me, and I want them to be safe from the fear I had to suffer, and not to die in that fear."

I was surprised at the flood of anger her words carried, and the silence that followed carried all she had implied. Wasn't she speaking to her Uncle Henri? Wasn't she reminding him that he too had chosen to remain in the safety of exile rather than risk his own neck as her parents had done, and even herself, for the king's cause?

The marquis's face whitened, I thought, and Jean's had taken on a haunted look, and I watched as Michel began to peel his fruit with thick, stubby fingers.

But it was Charette who said, "Well, apparently the king's cause is not dead, however Michel would believe it. We all are aware of it, aren't we?" Her words belied the sweetness in her voice, that cloying sweetness I should always connect with her. "It's clear that Nicolas is rising to that cause, and the police are anxious to track him down. I wonder that you don't put a stop to it, Uncle Honoré. Is not your first allegiance to General Bonaparte, for didn't you take the oath, in order to have the château and the title returned to you? Maurice said that you owe everything to our new first consul. You are even among those invited to attend the receptions he gives at the Tuileries in Paris, although you never attend. Maurice said that Jean should show more respect, and join forces with Bonaparte. He would be given an immediate commission if he took the colors. Maurice said—"

"The devil take what Maurice said, Charette!" Jean exploded, throwing down his napkin and standing up. He left the table and stalked from the room. Charette had turned pale, her lower lip trembling, and she suddenly jumped up and fled from the room like a naughty child.

The marquis looked abashed, Michel seemed unmoved, and Danielle was more distressed than ever. Yet I could find no words to comfort her.

Shortly afterward I excused myself and went to bed although it was quite early, more exhausted than ever before. A world and a whole lifetime seemed to have come and gone in the past forty-eight hours, and I had emerged a different woman.

To my surprise I was successful in teaching Aimée quite a bit of English, far more than I'd thought I could. The little girl responded easily enough, and within the week I had her speaking several sentences which she took pride in showing off to her family. She was a delightful child, with a winning charm that made my hours spent with her pleasant and fulfilling, although much of what I felt was due to the state of happiness I was living in with Jean.

Only Charette seemed to look upon my accomplishments as foolish ones. I learned quickly that she had no patience or liking whatsoever for Aimée, but I believed that was because she felt Aimée had usurped her place as the adored one in the household. It was she who often referred to Aimée as "Danielle's bastard," although she was careful not to say it around those who would slap her for it, I noticed.

One morning Jean came to me and said quietly, "Would you care to ride with me out along our coast, Tamar? I want to show you something special."

"Of course. I'd love to go."

Danielle warned me, "I hope you know how to ride, my dear. Knowing that coastline, it is rugged and can be very dangerous when you aren't familiar with it."

"I know how to ride," I said, almost revealing that I'd even been there a few nights back, but Jean intervened. "She will be safe with me, Danielle, so you must not worry so." He touched her arm in a gesture meant to reassure her. She only nodded, and I went up to change into my habit.

I hurried into the dark amber velvet which Neville had chosen for me; I had not yet worn it, and when I surveyed myself in the mirror, I felt transformed. I was suddenly very glad, too, that

Charette was not present, knowing she was with the marquis who had taken her to Brest earlier, for I was certain she would have asked Jean if she could come along.

When I returned to the hall where Jean was waiting, I believed I saw admiration in his eyes as he appraised my appearance. We were alone. Jean held me at arm's length, then without a word, kissed me gently on the lips and led me from the house into the stableyards.

Our mounts were all ready for us, and we rode out through the gates we had come in that first night, and started toward the village. It was another day of golden beauty; fields were deep with yellowed grasses and the sky was a blazing blue. We passed on the outskirts of the village around a high stone wall covered with roses still in bloom, and as we started down through a sloping vineyard, Jean began to talk.

"Tomorrow is the feast day of October first when the people of our village gather to start their harvesting. It is a small thing, but in the past it was an important event. There will be dancing and drinking of the new wine from this season's grapes. Michel has charge of that, bringing in the casks from the Farms," he explained. "Would you like to come? We don't have to stay but a little while, but it will give you an idea of what it was like here long ago." His voice held a wistfulness I couldn't miss, and I wanted desperately to learn about this man and his moods.

I turned and looked at him. "I should like it very much. It must bring back a lot of memories."

He nodded. "My parents loved to attend, but I

think it was my mother who enjoyed it most. She always made a big thing of it for us, taking Danielle and me when we were little, and allowing us to stay for the dancing when we were older. She and Danielle dressed in peasant skirts and blouses, and we all danced and danced. It was all so light and carefree then."

We rode on through the vineyard, which sloped upward toward the cliffs, and when we reached them, Jean stopped. For a moment we both just stared in awe at the timeless beauty of that seascape. Along the coast were copses of stunted pine trees bent by the Atlantic winds. Although there was a breeze today, it was gentle and moist on our faces, but the vivid green swell of the ocean mercilessly pounded the granite cliff walls below.

Jean called my attention to the ancient castle on a point of land that jutted out into the seething green sea. "It is an eleventh-century Norman fortress, one of many that our Anjouvian kings built for the defense of our coast," he said. "Now it is only a shell, and very dangerous to wander about in. The approach, of course, is what turns would-be interested parties away. The bridge over the moat has long since rotted away, and it is virtually impossible to get across."

I was entranced with the scene; it had that look of being woven into a tapestry, remote and untouchable. "I want to take you to the caves below them, Tamar," Jean said in a low voice.

"The caves?"

He nodded. "This region is a part of ancient *Armorica,* conquered by Caesar. The fugitive

Bretons gave us the name of Brittany long before those Norman kings came, and they hid in those deep salt caves along this coast. Those Bretons had a fierce and long struggle for independence, first from the Franks and then from the dukes of Normandy and the counts of Anjou."

"Where are those caves?"

"Come, I'll show you."

We followed a path right on the edge of the cliffs where the wind touched us, catching my hair and bringing it loose from its pins. I removed my hat and tucked it into the saddle pouch, and my hair swung free. Jean laughed as he looked back at me, and then we dipped down, the trail barely wide enough for one horse at a time.

There was an old saying that the higher one climbs, the greater the fall, but what did I care for sayings on that day? We laughed like children as we rode, the wind carrying our laughter on wings like the gulls soaring around us. We lost sight of the ancient fortress several times as our horses brushed wild gorse and yellowed broom, but when we finally came out on a rather flat cliff top, the castle was before us, across a deep chasm.

"It's a shame we can't roam through it," I said regretfully, knowing I had a natural inclination for exploring. "It's beautiful."

"Screech owls haunt it by night, and they say ghosts roam through its halls. I don't wonder, for I suspect there were many bloody battles fought here," Jean said quietly. "But let's dismount here." He swung easily to the ground and helped me down, and in that sweet moment his nearness overpowered me, and for an instant he held me to him, stroking my long windswept hair.

Then he went to tether the horses, and as he did so, I glanced around me. Thick brambles and ivy, touched with the changing red of autumn, entwined around everything. No wind struck here, as it seemed protected by a shelf of gray granite rock.

When Jean returned, he said, "Wait here one moment," and he plunged into that wild bramble. I glanced back to see where the horses were, but they too were hidden within the trees. This gave me a twinge of uneasiness I was unprepared for. I felt all alone. I did not hear a sound, save that of the gulls' mournful cries. I shivered as a sudden coldness came over me.

All at once there was a screech that startled me so violently that I jerked around, trembling, smothering a scream in my throat. It was only when I realized that a bird in the thicket had been disturbed by Jean that I laughed at myself. When he reappeared with a thick rope over his shoulders, he was laughing.

"That was one of those *chat-huant* nests, and I disturbed it," he explained. "The screech owl of Brittany. It is popular along these cliffs, and they make their nests near those caves. *Voilà,* but she gave me such a scare!" He laughed again, and my relief was immense, but I still felt more than a little shaky.

"The *Chouans* have taken their name from that owl, Tamar," he said quietly, looking at my face. "They use that call, and the old *chevalier* spirit is aroused. I'm sure when most people around here hear that screech owl in the night, they do not rest in their beds."

I shuddered. "And it is all starting again," I murmured, disturbed, knowing and remembering the anguish with which Danielle had spoken out that night. I thought I knew why she could feel so bitterly about men and their strange dreams of war.

Jean shifted the heavy ropes on his shoulder. "Come along. Follow me carefully," and he turned and walked down through a hidden trail in the brambles, with me hurrying behind him. When we came out suddenly on a small granite ledge, he dropped the ropes over the ledge, and I saw at once it was a ladder of sorts. He secured the ends of it around the base of a strong tree, and then turned to me.

"Don't worry. It's not far down, and it's not dangerous if you go carefully. We only go down to that wide ledge. I'll go first. Are you sure you want to go?" He was testing my courage, daring me with a challenge, I thought.

"Try me. It will be exciting." And with that he started down the ladder. When he called up to me to start down, I hitched up my skirts and stepped down as he had done. I moved carefully, and felt his strong hands around my waist when I reached the bottom. We both laughed. "You need boy's breeches if you intend to climb around very often!"

I glanced down at my habit and burst out laughing. "No doubt you're right, but this is the best I have at the moment." He reached over and brushed some dust from my leg. Then we turned our attention to what was before us. The sound of water was closer here, like a dull roar, and as Jean pointed down over the ledge we were standing on, I saw the reason.

"When the tide is low, it is easy to cross this moat by a rope bridge farther along here. The caves are over there, under the fortress. Some of them are over here, around this bend. Come, I'll show you."

I could see that this was a natural defense route. If the enemy once gained knowledge of it, that fortress could be taken. I walked alongside Jean, glad he was with me, but all the same I felt uneasy. I could not shrug off the sensation that we were being watched, and I wondered if Jean felt it too, for he was exceptionally watchful, and kept his voice low.

The thick leaves and vines that trailed over the cliff were scarlet and yellow, and served as a colorful curtain. Suddenly Jean pushed aside these thick vines and peered into what was an opening in the thick wall of granite. He went in, then after a moment motioned for me to follow him.

5

At once, the musty smells of earth hit us. The dull roar of the sea was present, and a chill of the ages clung to the granite walls. Jean stood quite still, then reached out to a ledge and found what he knew would be there, short ends of tallow and flint, one of which he immediately lit, placing another in his jacket pocket. Then he thrust the light into my hand and lit another one, holding it up.

Something caused my heart to flutter oddly, like a warning, for in the yellowish garish light, for the briefest of seconds, his face had a satyr-like expression and his eyes shone like a cat's.

"We'll follow a narrow tunnel now into the larger caves, and we'll need some light. It's not really far, but it will give you an impression of what use these caves have seen through the centuries." The sound of his voice gave me a profound sense of relief. "Follow me closely through this part." He moved with swiftness into the darker hole, and I had to hurry to keep up with him.

The warm air that touched us when we reached the first cave surprised me. Jean explained, "You can see why these were perfect abodes for those earlier people. There is a warm current of air that drifts through here, and the floor of the caves is sandy and dry. Suddenly we plunged into a very narrow tunnel. "We're going under the moat now, Tamar. In the past, these caves we're going to see now were where all the contraband salt was hidden from the tax collectors. The Cottereau brothers were the instigators, but my grandfather and my father were not to be outdone by them, and offered their land, using these caves and the Rouvroy rights to them. This fortress still is on Rouvroy land. Hardly anyone ever knew about the caves. So it was natural that the *Chouans* used them as their lair, and their hiding place. They stored their arms and provisions, living out precarious lives. Those are the *chevaliers* with whom I have now joined forces." He spoke grimly, I thought at once.

As he finished speaking, we came to the end of the tunnel, and taking three steps up, we came into what looked like an antechamber of sorts. It was large, oblong, and at the other end of the room I could see a stone staircase.

"Were these caves ever discovered by the Revolutionists, or by General Hoche and his men?"

He shook his head. "No, and that is why we can still use them now," he said, and gazed around us. "This is but a chamber under the fortress; there are dungeons here that would make those in our château look like pleasure rooms, believe me. But they are dangerously in ruins. You have no particular fancy to see them, do you?" He cocked an eyebrow at me, and I had a glimpse of the old mocking amusement in his smile and in the way he looked at me.

I shook my head. "I believe you, and that is enough," I said quickly, and he laughed. "Is this the castle Charette wanted to ride to with you?" I recalled that morning when she'd dashed out into the courtyard, asking him to ride out with her.

He seemed to hesitate before he answered, as if he wanted to choose his words, and I believed in that moment I saw something in his expression that told me he did not like to be reminded of Charette.

"Charette likes to ride out here, and she does so when she gets the chance. But," he said as he took my hand and led me toward a door in the rock wall, "forget that. Forget Charette. I want to take you into the grotto, into the other caves. They are special, you'll see."

We stepped through the door, and it was a totally different world. Jean took my light and snuffed it out along with his, for here we did not need the candles. Daylight poured in from great arches to the west, giving an ethereal glow to the water beneath the dome of gray-white rock. Again I had the sensation we were not alone; he sensed my fears, for he suddenly pulled me closer to him. "There are small boats here." He pointed to several tied up to the natural stone quay that had been used for centuries. "We'll take one and row through the grotto where we'll come to the main caves." He spoke in a hushed voice, but it seemed to echo back, and I shivered in spite of myself.

"There's nothing to be frightened of. There are still very few who know of this place. It is safe." And he helped me down into the small boat and untied the rope, then settled himself down to the oars.

It was a beautiful place. The water was deep here, still and dark. In my mind's eye I tried to visualize those fugitives coming here, hiding, and I tried to imagine Jean's parents and Danielle there.

Jean steered the boat through the stalacites jutting from the roof of the grotto like twisted columns, and rowed up to the rock-hewn quay. "This is often called the grotto of robbers, for only robbers have ever lived here," Jean said as he helped me from the boat. "You're still not afraid?" He lifted his brows.

I shook my head. "No. It is—eerie, but I want to see." I could have told him my curiosity often overcame fears in the very worst of situations.

"Come then. We'll hurry, for we don't want to be caught after dark. They'll wonder what became of you at the château if I don't bring you back for dinner."

I walked beside him into the caves, and it was there I saw the kegs and casks of arms and provisions. I saw discarded papers and jars of food, and knew at once that this had to be the place where Nicolas had hidden from the police. Jean gazed around, and for the first time it occurred to me that he had made the excuse to bring me here so he could see for himself what had been done with his cargo.

I said, "This place must not be far from where your ship is anchored." But he only nodded, and I went on, "All these casks—you brought them all from England?"

"Yes. They are filled with guns and ammunition."

"I see. Then Nicolas is hiding out here?"

"It seems the likely place for him to be, yes." And I wondered again why Nicolas had been at the convent that afternoon. I mentioned it to Jean as he went over to stand beside a table spread with a rough map of sorts. There were other signs of Nicolas's living there: a straw mattress in one corner and blankets folded neatly on it; a kettle over an iron grill; dry wood in a box nearby; pewter cups and plates stacked on a roughly made shelf above the table beside a large lantern.

"I was surprised to know Nicolas was at the convent, too," Jean said slowly, "but then, he has an aunt who is one of the sisters there. They are very devout Catholics, the Cottereau family." He was studying the map, and I came to stand beside him. He pulled me to him, his eyes dark on mine as he turned my face to look at me. He began to kiss me, so gently that I just melted into him, and then more and more deeply until an incredible weakness overcame my body and my senses began to whirl. I scarcely was conscious of it when he lifted me in his arms and carried me to the straw mattress and knelt beside me, pressing me back to the straw.

"I've wanted to be alone with you," he said, and

he pressed his lips in the hollow of my throat. I knew only a sense of wanting it too, and in the tiny moment before I was drowned in a sensuous desire for his kisses, I wondered if this was how Danielle felt when she had met my brother.

Our passions rose as we continued to explore our love, kissing and touching ever so gently. I was beginning to feel as if we were the only two creatures on earth, when an ear-splitting screech resounded through the caves, striking terror in my heart so that I trembled violently and sat up. Jean jerked away and stood up, startled as I was, just as the figure in brown leather appeared in the entrance of the cave.

It was Nicolas. He leaned against the wall watching us boldly, taking in my rumpled riding skirt and tousled hair. I turned from that stare, my face scarlet, and hurriedly began to smooth my clothes with angry trembling fingers. Jean stood between the door and me.

"I should have knocked, *mon ami,*" laughed Nicolas. "The chevalier and his lady shouldn't have been interrupted, eh?" How deep and sonorous his laugh was, and as Jean drew me to my feet, I saw the confident look on his face that said, "Say nothing, Tamar. I will take care of it."

Jean laughed. "We did not expect you, Nicolas. Have you been out to the Point?" Obviously, he was not going to make an issue out of it by making explanations to this man.

"The coast is swarming with Labbé's men," Nicolas laughed, sauntering in and taking a tobacco pouch from his jacket. He took a pipe and lit it, and I glimpsed the gun in his belt, realizing that he would not hesitate to use that weapon. "Monsieur Labbé is thickheaded, blind with power, but he is a persistent cuss that will stop at nothing to get revenge. I hear they have combed *L'Angélique* for any suspicious cargo."

Jean pulled my hand through his arm. "He found nothing, of course, and I was there to confront him. Still, it's a threat, Nicolas, and we've got to watch our next steps carefully. This will cool down in a few weeks' time, and they will call off their watchdogs. If you can stay out of sight until then, our mission will be safe enough." The two men eyed each other.

"I hear the marquis is getting ready to go to Paris very soon. The 'royal invitation' command from the Corsican is extended to all the repatriates, eh, Jean? Will you be going?" His eyes went from Jean to me, then back, as he leaned against the table crossing his arms. That insolent smile of his was not lost on Jean or myself, and I knew a certain stiffening of Jean's body next to mine.

"Where did you hear that, I wonder? It came only this morning."

Nicolas laughed, then said, "Don't fret so. My Uncle Michel keeps nothing to himself. Oh, yes," he smiled, seeing Jean's expression of surprise, "I've been in to see that uncle of mine. I had to do it sometime or other, and today seemed appropriate enough." He had a devil-may-care manner about him that made me uneasy, and Jean wasn't giving him any information whatsoever.

"Then I won't have to warn you he is opposed to what is being planned?" Jean said harshly.

Nicolas shrugged. "He has what he set out to

have. The man has gone soft, and he is not one of us, nor can he be trusted. I believe I have convinced him, however, that I was not in on the robbery he is so concerned with, and told him I've simply taken advantage of the first consul's amnesty toward repatriates."

I felt Jean's hand tighten on my arm as we began to walk out of the caves toward the quay. Nicolas followed us, and stood watching with that obnoxious grin on his face, and I realized I hadn't spoken a word to the man, nor had he spoken to me. Even the relationship between Jean and Nicolas seemed different in this visit than it was before, and I wondered why they seemed more like enemies than allies.

It was only when we reached our mounts that Jean turned to me, took me by the shoulders and brought me around to face him. "Listen, Tamar. You must be careful. You must promise me that you will be careful around Nicolas. Don't trust him. He is like—a viper, and he will strike when least expected. Yes. We are friends, but I know him. Trust me, will you? Promise me."

"Of course," I said, entirely in the dark as to the reason for his warning. He kissed my lips gently, held me to him for a brief moment, and then released me. I wanted to ask him questions, but I guessed there would be time for that, and when we mounted our horses, I was quite content to ride alongside him, our thoughts now occupied with each other. We wandered the cliffs, taking our time, lost in each other's company, and it was dusk before we rode back to the château.

We watched the sun set on the sea, holding

hands as the flaming copper and pink disk sank into the mysterious horizon; we slowly made our way down through the vineyards and past the village walls and back to the château. The magic of that day still lingered and I suppose our joy showed clearly in our faces when we arrived, quite late, and went to our rooms to change for dinner.

I soaped my skin and washed in a bath of warm scented water, then wrapped myself in the huge towel and put on fresh undergarments. Lili had laid out a deep blue silk gown, and I was brushing the tangles from my hair when Charette came in abruptly without knocking, closing the door behind her. I turned around on the small stool I was sitting upon and stared at her.

"You went riding out with Jean this afternoon, didn't you?"

Still in a haze of love, I smiled at her. "Yes. Of course."

"He—he took you to the castle, didn't he?"

I stared at her, quietly brushing the ends of my curls around my fingers. "Yes. It's a most romantic place, that old castle. Remote, mysterious, but so beautifully romantic." Yet something inside me warned me of her questions. I sat back and studied her face calmly. For one so young, and I knew now she was eighteen, she seemed ripe and ready to plunge into a marriage bed. With this thought, I felt my skin tingle with shame, knowing I too had wished for that during the hours spent with Jean that very afternoon. These thoughts ran through my mind, and I almost felt naked as I saw her eyes move over my face as if she could see in them what had happened in the caves.

I turned back to my mirror.

"He took you to the caves, didn't he?"

The brush dropped from my hand, clattering on the tabletop, and I let it lie there while I began to pin up my curls rather quickly.

"You are being rather inquisitive," I said, trying to smile, but she came up and stood behind me, looking over my shoulder. There was a curious look of malice and envy in the black eyes reflected in the mirror.

I didn't want to blatantly hurt her, nor did I want to discuss where I'd been with Jean during my magical day. This was something one did not share, not with a jealous rival.

"Those were *our* caves, and *our* castle," she said suddenly, angrily, her breath coming too quickly. "You are not to go there again with him, ever!" she cried. "You can't have him! I won't let you. Jean is mine! He's mine, do you hear? You don't belong here. I don't believe a single word of his rescuing you from pirates, or that he wants to marry you!"

I stood up. "You are making a spectacle of yourself, Charette," I began, hoping to calm her down, and I walked over to where my gown lay. "Indeed, you are making one horrible mistake, and you don't understand what you are saying."

"Oh, yes I do!" She whirled toward me, her face contorted with hate.

I lifted my gown, ignoring her, but she flew at me, jerked the gown from my hand, and in one incredible, malicious act, she ripped the bodice in half. Flinging it down on the floor, she stomped on it, her tiny French heels tearing the beautiful fabric. More astonished than anything, I reached out and slapped her face hard, the marks of my fingers scarlet on her cheek.

"You think yourself engaged to him, but I know better. I know all about what has been going on—the plans to get the Englishman here—and you're his sister! You both are only pretending, but you want him!" She came close to me, her dislike of me so disturbing that I was almost frightened. Her voice rose. "I won't let you have my Jean, I won't! I'm warning you, stay away from Jean!"

There was a shocking silence, and before I could say anything in my defense, Danielle appeared at the entrance of my dressing room, her face revealing that she had heard everything. Lili was behind her.

"Charette." The girl whirled around, taken by surprise. "I think you had better apologize—"

"No!" she shrieked. "I will not. You . . . you will take her part, because you want to please Jean, but I found out that she is a spy! Jean is not in love with her! He could never—not her. . . ." The resounding slap of Danielle's hand across the girl's cheek stopped Charette's words, reducing her to an uncontrollable sobbing.

"You had better go to your room, Charette. Lili, please take this torn gown to Madame Hortense, and see if anything can be done to repair it." Charette turned and ran from the room, and Danielle looked at me.

"This is truly inexcusable. I'm afraid this has

gone too far now. Will you be all right, my dear? I will go to her." She bit her lip, as unhappy as I was about the whole affair.

"Yes. Of course," I said, still trembling from the emotions the girl had aroused within me. I watched the maid leave with my gown and knew with a certainty I would never wear it, not after this.

Danielle touched my arm, imploring me to be patient and forgiving. "She must not be allowed to continue this possessiveness of Jean, Tamar. Somehow we are all responsible, and she must be taken in hand. I wish Maurice would come for a while. He knows how to—well, to talk to her." But she spoke as if she were speaking to herself, and then she pressed my hand. "I will go to her now." She smiled sadly at me, and after I assured her I was fine, she left me.

I returned to my dressing, more uneasy than ever. All I could think of—now that love's rosy glow was gone—was Charette's wild emotions, her infatuation with Jean.

Her discovery of the plot to get my brother here had surprised me, yet it is what I should have expected. Had she learned it from Jean on that first day when he'd taken her aside? I wondered what he had told her; had it been the truth? I thought of all that had transpired since that day, but I could not doubt Jean's love for me or, for that matter, my own love for Jean. Not after those brief but perfect moments alone today.

But there had been something unmistakably desperate in Charette's accusations. A tiny serpent of fear began to uncoil deep within me, as I brought out another gown from the cupboard, a dark green velvet with ecru lace at the neckline and the elbows. It was a flattering dress and gave me needed self-confidence.

Impulsively I brought out the locket and weighed it in my mind as well as in my hands. This belonged to Danielle, I thought. It would probably bring back painful memories to her. I decided that I should wait for the time when I could show it to her without fear of hurting her. First I wanted to learn how it had been taken to Columb Manor. So I replaced it among my very personal things to await a better time.

When I left my rooms, I decided to go along to look in on Aimée, as had become my habit as well as a pleasure, before she went to sleep. Her rooms were in the other wing, down the corridor from the apartments Danielle shared with her husband.

Aimée was not there. I walked through her small dressing room into the bedroom and, although her bed was turned back and the candles were burning brightly on the mantelpiece, there was no sign of the child.

I heard a faint sound; it was slight, but enough to raise goose pimples on my skin. I was staring at the curtained alcove beside the bed, and because I was standing quite close, I saw the bulge behind it. My heart thumped madly, and when a face peered out between those curtains, I nearly fainted from sheer fright at the horrible mask-like image that leered out at me.

A peal of girlish laughter burst out from behind that mask, and a tiny form ran out, her nightgown billowing around her.

"Oh, mademoiselle!" she cried, taking off the mask. "You were so frightened, were you not?" She laughed mischievously.

"What on earth—" I cried, looking at the red devil's face with horns and black holes for its eyes. My hands were still trembling. "Where did it come from? Why do you have such a horrible thing?" I calmed myself and was able to smile in spite of myself.

"It's a devil's mask, mademoiselle. One of the mummers who will be at the village feast tomorrow came to visit *maman* today, and he left his mask here for me to play with. Is it not frightening? *Maman* says she will take me to the village tomorrow if I am a good little girl. I will be good. I promise."

"Then I think you can begin by getting in bed, don't you? It's long past your bedtime." I glanced around in the charming room fixed up prettily in pastel pinks and blues.

"I waited for you to come, Mademoiselle Tamar. *Maman* said you might not come, but I wished for you to come so I could scare you with my devil." She laughed, and I smiled at her as she climbed onto the bed. "Did I truly frighten you with it?" She looked at me expectantly, and I tucked her in under the coverlet.

"Of course you did. I was frightened out of my wits! Does that make you happy?"

"It really is supposed to make people laugh, I think," she said wisely. "I wouldn't want to *really* scare you. Not to make you cry. Just to make you laugh."

"That is a very sensible way of looking at it," I

said, kissing her cheek. I glanced up as the maid came in and watched me. I said, "Good-night, little one. Sleep tight, for we both shall certainly enjoy the festival with all those scary mummers."

Her face was radiant. "Oh, mademoiselle! You are going with us too, *n'est-ce pas?*"

"And what could keep me away? Mariane," I said, smiling at the maid who looked after Aimée, "you would not keep me away from the festival, now would you?" I winked at her.

"*Non, non,* mademoiselle, not I!" she exclaimed wide-eyed. Aimée giggled and wrinkled her pert little nose.

I laughed and blew a kiss to her, saying, "Take care of our little mummer, Mariane. See to it that she gets her beauty sleep."

"*Oui,* mademoiselle, *oui.*" And I left them, closing the door softly behind me.

Dinner that evening was a strained affair, for Danielle had insisted that Charette make a formal apology to me for her irrational attack. Even the marquis was shocked at her behavior. Before the dinner was halfway through, I saw that he had no patience with her sullen attitude, and sent her to her rooms.

It was a most trying time, distressing for the family more than for me, and Jean had been not much help throughout the ordeal. He had remained silent and aloof to the girl who had sent him pleading messages from her dark glances. While in a way I was glad, I found his attitude somewhat cold and uncaring. Surely she had once meant something to him, or she would not have such a fierce attachment to him. If nothing else, they were still cousins.

The tension lessened somewhat after her departure, and it was while we were being served our after-dinner coffee and chocolate-covered mints that Jean abruptly said, "We want to announce our engagement, and as soon as possible." He spoke directly to the marquis, who looked at me curiously, a silent question in his expression. "Perhaps we can have a talk with the curé tomorrow. We've decided on an early wedding."

Danielle seemed surprised, as did Michel, who had been very uncommunicative all evening, frowning deeply but saying nothing.

"If you're both sure, I can't see what should stop you, Jean," she said gently. "It could be done easily enough. How early is *early* for you?" Her smile was dazzling. I could almost see how she was thinking; that this would surely hasten a positive action whereby Charette would have to come to terms with her infatuation, but I was not sure it was the answer.

"Within the month—a fortnight, if possible," Jean said, startling even me. I too wanted an early wedding, now that our feelings had been declared. But two weeks . . .

"So soon?" the marquis asked.

"We see no further reason to wait, since we've had some communication from Tamar's brother. Perhaps a ball and the wedding could be combined?" I thought I saw an anxious look of desire in Jean's eyes when he looked at me, and knew he, too, longed for greater pleasures.

"Of course. If that is how you want it, I'm sure

it can be arranged," the marquis said. "I might mention to you, Jean, to remember the mandatory invitation, the imperial command that I attend the Tuileries Reception within the month."

"I haven't forgotten," Jean said quietly.

"I believe you have been invited too." The marquis took a deep breath, and looked at Michel. "The summons came after mine did, while you were away this afternoon."

"Mon Dieu!" Jean exploded. "How the devil did that happen?" I saw the twist of angry contempt on his lips.

The marquis's mouth tightened in just the same manner. "I think we know the answer to that. Bonaparte still knows we are the Rouvroys, a part of the old aristocratic power he has passionately endeavored to win to his side. We could carry a great deal of weight if we chose to fight on his side, my son. Especially now that there is so much resistance flaring up in the provinces. We are to be watched and coddled. I don't like it."

"Neither do I," Jean said darkly.

Michel said, "Why not give him what he demands? Surely if he deems it an honor to invite you, you should respect that. That he has chosen to test your loyalty should be easy enough to accept. You have everything to gain. I should consider it a privilege to have such an invitation." He spoke with an underlying bitterness. He knew he would never be invited to attend Bonaparte's reception, although he was more deserving of such an honor than Jean or the marquis, if loyalty were to be counted. It must have galled him.

The hard brown eyes of the marquis turned on Michel. They were contemptuous to say the least, but he said, "Would that you could go in my place, Michel." Then he looked at Jean. "But whether we go or not depends on several things. I've not made up my mind yet. I wanted to discuss it further with you, Jean, as one of us will have to go. God knows, what with Maurice in his army, you'd think the general's appetite would be appeased, but no! He is a greedy fool!"

Danielle spoke quietly, her face white. "Perhaps Jean should go in your behalf, and Tamar could go along? She might like a chance to buy a wedding dress. Madame Bonaparte sets such a fashion in Paris that it might be easy to find a gown." I know she was thinking of the gown her cousin had destroyed.

"That is an excellent idea, Danielle," the marquis said. "Jean? Does that not sound all right? You could stay at the town house, for Marcel managed to keep four rooms for our use when Bonaparte confiscated the house. I understand the house is now used as flats, so Marcel writes. What do you say, Jean?"

"We shall consider it, I think," Jean said slowly, giving me a look that said we would discuss it together, alone. It occurred to me how we could read each other's eyes so well in such a short time; but then it seemed as if I had known Jean for all my life.

"Bon," the marquis said, and rang for champagne to be brought so we could celebrate the coming ball and wedding.

Some time later, Jean and I left together and

walked out into the garden. Darkness was falling, and there were stars in the sky. We walked in a silence that was warm and close, and for a time I just marveled at our happiness.

Then Jean turned to me. "I've never seen you look more beautiful than you are tonight, Tamar. I'm glad, aren't you? I mean, that we will hurry with our plans to be married? It is what you wish too, *n'est-ce pas?*" His eyes were filled with tenderness, and I could feel his pulse leap beneath my fingers as I touched his arm.

"Yes, of course." I couldn't help the rapid beating of my own heart. I swallowed hard, for I knew that one thing would complete my happiness and that was to have my brother see me in this joy, and to have him give us his blessings.

"You have no doubts, do you?"

"No."

He lifted my hand to his warm lips. "You do love me, Tamar? I know you do. I felt it in you today, in the caves—"

"Yes. I love you, Jean."

"Then we must plan. Would you like to go to Paris with me? We could make a gala affair of it, if you wish. Have you been to Paris before?"

I shook my head. "No. Never. I . . . I have always longed to go there."

"It is a city of light and beauty, and I would love to show it to you for the first time. Perhaps we could even persuade Danielle to come with us? She would like it."

"That would make it even more delightful," I said, smiling. "But would Michel mind very much? I seemed to detect a slight air of possessiveness in his attitude toward her. He might not like it."

"It's true, of course, but what the devil can he do about it if she wants to go with us? It will do her good to get away from him. Besides, I believe Danielle was planning on a little visit there sometime soon. You know, don't you, how sorry we all are that Charette was so uncharitable to act as she did? Danielle was saying to me that we must make amends somewhere for her attack. What a little hellion she turned out to be!"

We stood together in the shadows, and Jean placed his hands on my shoulders. In the yellow light of the lanterns over the arbor we stood in, his face looked darker than usual. It was I who said, "You have not been . . . playing fast and loose with her emotions, have you, Jean? I have to know, you see. She . . . she has such a fixation about you, and I would not want to deliberately flaunt . . ." I stopped, seeing his expression when he placed a finger over my lips.

"You are not to presume that I took advantage of that child, Tamar. She is a sensitive person, truly likable underneath all that fire and jealousy. I believe she took one incident to mean a great deal more than it truly was, that's all, and built it up in her mind. Because she was lonely, I befriended her when she needed me. She never had a mother, and I was more like a friend than a cousin. I gave her more attention than was necessary perhaps. But she is not the woman in my heart or in my life. You must see that and know it. Do you, my darling Tamar? Do you know that?"

He was serious, anxious that I should know it. "I think I do, yes. What was the incident . . . she took to mean more than it was? Perhaps I should know—"

He took a deep breath. "It was nothing. I merely kissed her once, when we were out riding."

"At the castle?" I prompted.

He nodded. "But it was nothing more than the affection of one cousin for another. You must believe me. Don't let her tantrums cloud our horizon. Let's you and I help her, and we can do this best now by proving that we are to be married, and that I am in love with you."

I smiled, and his lips touched mine gently. "Yes. Of course. I want to help her know that. But Jean," I frowned, my voice low. "She said something that made me uneasy, and I think you should know."

"And what is that?" He didn't seem interested, but embraced me, and I found his caresses distracting.

"She said she knew I was a spy—that she knew all about the plot to bring my brother, the Englishman, over here. I suppose you told her this?" He suddenly stiffened. He looked at me seriously.

"Where on earth could she have learned that? No, of course I didn't tell her."

We were silent for a moment and then I said, "Have you ever taken her to the caves, Jean?"

"Why do you ask this? I don't believe she even knows the caves exist, or if she does, I'm sure she hasn't been there. Not with me."

I tried to look away, but I couldn't. "She mentioned something about the caves being her

. . . private ones, and wanted to know if you'd taken me there today. She was very possessive about them." I tried to laugh, but I felt rather shaken instead, and Jean didn't smile.

"Then someone has taken her, and she knows too many things that she shouldn't know!" he said, letting out a heavy sigh. "I have my suspicions—" He stopped, but not before I'd heard the anger in his voice. Looking down at me, he shrugged.

"I'm afraid this wretched affair has left us all touchy and rather exhausted. Shall we go inside now? I'll put it to Danielle tomorrow about going to Paris with us. And I'll speak to the curé of our parish and we can make our plans from there."

When we returned to the house, we found Danielle had already retired, and the marquis seemed to be waiting for Jean. I sensed he wished a word with him alone, so I made my excuses and went along to my rooms. But although I undressed and put on my chemise and pink wrapper, I did not go immediately to bed, but sat for a while at the open window. A scent of earthiness and heavy dew stole in from the gardens, and the sound from the sea was a sibilant whisper in the night.

I had been at the château for nearly a fortnight, and because I had been so lost in my own cloud of happiness I hardly had noticed the passage of time. It seemed as if my former life had never been, and I tried to remember what it was like at Columb Manor, and what was happening there, but I could not. There had been no word from my brother, but I knew with a surety that he would plan his act with preciseness whenever the time was right. I knew Neville, and I had no doubts that he would come for me.

When I questioned Jean, I sensed that he was reluctant to speak of it. "The less you know of this whole affair, Tamar," he'd said, "the better. I'm determined to not let any danger touch either you or Danielle. Your brother will come." And he would say no more.

I woke up the next morning to find Aimée perched on the end of my bed, asking me if I was going to be lazy and not get up on this very important day. I glanced at the clock on the mantel and saw that it was half-past ten already, and she bubbled with excitement over being allowed to go to the festival. "But *maman* will not let me stay for the play-acting in the evening," she said, pouting a little.

"I should hope not," I cried, with mocking horror. "It's not for little girls' eyes and ears, with all those devil masks and such. Besides, you would be bored and wouldn't like it." I laughed, and got out of bed. "Oh, but I am late this morning! What on earth made me sleep so late? And our lessons! We must get to them, or we shall not get to go at all!"

While I rushed through my toilette with Aimée chattering like a magpie and following me from room to room, Lili brought in a tray with hot croissants and a pot of chocolate. She, too, was excited, as she was going to the festival as well.

It was Danielle who came looking for Aimée, and found us both eating the croissants. I had not yet dressed, for I did not know what I should wear to such an occasion, and when I saw Danielle's peasant skirt and blouse with a black, laced bodice, I became excited. Over her arm she carried another set of clothes, and laid them down across the chair.

"It's traditional to wear the local peasant garb to such an affair," she said when she saw my expression. "I brought you these. Here is a scarf like the one I'm wearing, Tamar. When you've dressed, I'll show you how to tie it over your hair so it won't come off." Of course I couldn't help but admire the gay look about her, the smiling lustrous eyes, and dazzling grin. "We've planned a family picnic, and we're leaving within the hour."

"A picnic, *maman*? Shall I go change too?" Aimée nearly shrieked with joy, and Danielle said, "Oh, yes. Come along, my poppet. Our Tamar must have time to dress, and we don't want to keep the others waiting." Without another word, Aimée scampered down from the chair beside me and took her mother's hand obediently, and I could not fail to smile at the child's delight over a picnic. I caught her excitement too, for I felt like being free, dressed as a peasant, and being with the one I loved.

"We'll be ready in about an hour's time, my dear," Danielle said. "It's all very impromptu, mind you, but Jean is very anxious to show you the old way of life in our village."

I said, my heart trembling joyously, "I feel so very fortunate. I think it is a marvelous idea."

She leaned over and touched my cheek with her hand. "Bless you, Tamar dear. You are good for him, you know. He has a certain lightness of mind, which I am sure comes from his heart. I've noticed the difference, and I'm glad you are here."

I didn't need to ask what the difference was; I already knew, so I only smiled and she left with Aimée skipping beside her through the door.

I had hardly dressed in the deep burgundy skirt bordered with embroidered flowers, laced the black bodice tightly, and gone in search of Danielle to help me with the scarf than a visitor arrived, causing tremendous excitement. Aimée was at the window when a clatter of horses' hooves sounded in the courtyard.

"It's Maurice, *maman!*" she cried, jumping up and down. "He's come home to us!" Danielle rushed to the window, her face all smiles as she looked out and waved a greeting. *"Mon Dieu, mais oui!* This is the answer!" She turned to me with a look of relief on her face. "It's Charette's brother. Come. Let's go down and meet him. It will make our day happier, I think."

The young officer had just stepped into the hall when we hurried down the stairs, and Charette, exquisite in her peasant attire, skimmed past us and flew into his arms. Both Jean and the marquis were smiling as they entered the hall, just as pleasantly surprised as Danielle had been.

"Maurice!" cried Charette, her eyes dancing with pleasure at this handsome young man, dashing in the green and gold uniform. "How magnificent you look!"

"It's good to see you, Charette. And how pretty you are today. Is it because Jean has come home?"

She laughed and blushed, but there was a small strained silence as Maurice lifted his eyes to Jean and the marquis. The latter slapped the young captain on the shoulder in fond greeting, welcoming him home.

"So you've been made captain, eh? *Vraiment*, you're going up the ranks, my boy." They laughed and I had to remember that Maurice was his own son, as was Charette his daughter.

"It's not hard to do in these times, Uncle," he laughed, and turned to greet Danielle. "You grow prettier each time I see you, cousin. Like a young girl you are! And what is this occasion, dressed like . . . peasants?" His brown eyes were merry, and fell on Aimée, who was standing by and gazing rapturously at the gold-tasseled sash and saber that hung from his belt. "Of course! I forgot—today is the feast day! How wonderful!" Danielle laughed, and as he lifted Aimée in his arms so fondly, everyone crowded around and chattered about the festivities that were planned.

Then his eyes fell on me, and Jean came swiftly to my side, taking my hand.

"You have not met my fiancée, Maurice. May I present Mademoiselle Tamar Columb. Maurice, as you can see, is Charette's brother," he said to me.

"Your fiancée, eh?" He set Aimée down, and the bold brown eyes so like his sister's took me in in one appraising glance. Then he reached over and took my hand. "I didn't know, Jean." A dark flush touched his tanned cheeks as he kissed my hand. "*Enchanté*, mademoiselle. Maurice de Rouvroy at your service." He laughed, then pulled me to him and kissed my cheek. "Congratulations are in order, I suppose, Jean?" he said. "You have a most enchanting prize, *mon ami*."

"I know I have," Jean said.

"And mademoiselle is also my governess," Aimée said. She teaches me English, *n'est-ce pas, maman?*"

Danielle laughed. "She's all that and more, I am glad to say."

"All the better for you, *ma chère petite*," Maurice laughed at the little girl whose smile was so disarming no one could resist her.

Charette placed her arm through her brother's quite possessively, and said with that sweetness, "Well, let's not stand here all day discussing what Jean's fiancée can do, Maurice. We are about to have our picnic before the village festival. You will be my escort, won't you? Oh, I do think you should wear your lovely uniform. You'll be the envy of everyone in sight."

The marquis said, "Yes, Maurice, show your colors, for I've been told Labbé is posting his men in every hamlet on this day to look for anyone suspicious, and our village is not to be passed over, it seems."

"Why?" asked Maurice. "Has there been trouble here?"

"The diligence from Rennes was robbed two weeks ago, and the culprits have not been caught. Monsieur Labbé is fiendishly searching every nook and cranny for suspects."

Charette, impatient to be gone, said, "We mustn't waste our time chattering like this, when we don't even know how long Maurice is going to be with us. I hope it is for a long spell."

"I'm being assigned to a new unit which is moving toward the Austrian campaign next month. But I shall be here for a week or more, and then go to Paris. The first consul is giving a reception at the Tuileries, and I must be there."

"A family affair, so it seems," remarked the marquis dryly, winking at Jean.

Maurice caught it, and said with more heat than he wished to show, I thought, "I've been given a special request from our general to relay on to you, Uncle Honoré. He wishes your presence at that reception, and it will bring more harm than you might imagine if you do not attend."

"So I've already been informed, my boy," the marquis said. "But for now, don't remind me of it. Let's forget it if we can for the rest of this day, and enjoy what freedom we do have."

6

The festival was a holiday for everyone, and it
was traditional for families to bring their picnic
baskets and share their food with everyone. Deli-
cious-smelling delicacies and sumptuous dessert
were placed on long trestle tables set up under
the trees at the edge of the village green in a
golden field just harvested.

It was a day to be remembered, and my heart
was giddy with the abandonment of a gypsy. I sa
beside Jean in the driver's seat of the carriage
we'd taken, with Jean driving the two sturdy
white horses. His nearness stimulated me, and I
was sure I made him smile in that carefree
manner.

Behind us, Aimée, on Maurice's lap, chattered
incessantly, Charette and Danielle on either side
of them. The marquis drove another wagon up
ahead of us with various members of the house
hold and the picnic baskets stuffed with foods of

all kinds. Michel had left to set up the wine casks under the trees.

Along the winding bumpy road we passed families singing and walking hand in hand, and we saw a wagonload of mummers, with their strange, distorted masks. When we arrived at the field and I saw the crowds of happy people, it was hard to believe that they'd been through dark years of violence and destruction, for now they were intent on enjoying themselves as they had in years past. The atmosphere was light, our spirits high.

Already, a carnival-like spirit held the crowds. There were men in what looked like tattered rags of bright-colored patches and outlandish costumes, wearing masks that covered their entire heads and pointed shoes with clown-like curled-up toes. They made bawdy jokes, danced to merry tunes played on flutes and concertinas.

The Rouvroy family was greeted with respect I noticed at once. Because of their aristocratic background and noble bearing, they seemed different from the common people, but everyone appeared quite pleased at their arrival.

The Cottereau family gathered about, and I couldn't help wondering if Nicolas would have the sense to stay away.

We filled our plates with food and sat on the grass in the warm sun. The golden wine we drank was potent, making us all relax. Aimée sat between Jean and me while Danielle sat nearby with Michel. Maurice had flung back his head and was laughing at a mummer's performance of a lewd dance. Both Jean and Maurice had taken off their jackets, and I'd never seen Jean look more hand-some and relaxed as he was that warm golden hour.

Then from nowhere, it seemed, a tall broad-shouldered man in a mummer's costume stood on the fringe of our group, watching the other mummer's attempts to amuse Aimée. I looked at him and was stunned when he turned his eyes on me. The mask was so much like that of the poor unfortunate little Jock, the man aboard Jean's ship, *L'Angélique,* that I was shaken for an instant.

He was staring at me from behind that mask, for I could see the eyes behind that ludicrously painted face. A queer pang struck me, for there was something familiar about him, about those eyes, and my heart gave one great lurch. I felt faint for an instant, and I put my head down on my arm. When I lifted my head again, the man had disappeared among the crowds.

"Are you all right?" Jean whispered, his hand on my arm. I looked up and met his eyes. They were warm and searching.

"Yes. Of course," I said, breathing deeply. It couldn't be my brother; no, I shook my head in disbelief, as if to shake my suspicion. It was impossible. It was my imagination.

"What is it?" he asked. "You look as if you'd seen a ghost."

"Did you see that mummer?"

"Which one?" he laughed. "There are so many."

I shook my head. "His mask was painted just like . . . just like Jock's face, with that smile. . . ."

Jean took my hand in his own. "It was only a

mask. That face is very common. It has been around for centuries and is used for many of the mummers' masks. I believe that is how Jock's own face was created, because of some mummer's mask, poor little devil."

Again I shuddered, remembering the sad little man. Jean pressed my hand and brought it to his lips. "Are you sure you're all right? You look a little pale."

"I'm all right. I just thought for one moment—" I didn't finish, for Aimée stood up and began to do a little jig to the merry light tune of a piper, making everyone laugh.

It was time for the afternoon dancing, for which participants would be awarded prizes. I forgot my uneasiness and watched as partners were being chosen. I was amazed when the marquis chose Danielle to be his partner.

"It's the custom for the marquis to open the dance," Jean explained. "And then he will hand his partner to another. Then, after a while, the real dancers stay on and try to outdance each other. Will you dance with me?" His dark eyes stirred with excitement and his smile challenged me.

"But I hardly think . . ." The musicians had already struck up the first bars of gay country music. "It's easy. Just follow me, and move to the music. Your feet will move right with the rest of us." I had seen Charette looking at Jean invitingly, and I guessed she had hoped that he would choose her, assuming I didn't know the dances. Before I had a chance to refuse, Jean pulled me by the hand into the already dancing couples.

It was unlike anything I had ever known in England, and although I did not know the steps at first, my feet did move to the music as if by magic. I was whirled around, passing Maurice and Charette and Danielle and the marquis, not to mention the scores of gaudily dressed women and men who would entertain us in the evening.

Michel took no part in the dances; it occurred to me that he'd been ill at ease on this occasion, as if he hadn't known just what was his rightful place; but I wondered if he minded that his wife was looking like a young girl, laughing and being swung around by other men, some of them flirting with her outrageously.

There were mummers among us too, and when, from the corner of my eye, I saw the marquis hand Danielle over to one of them, a feeling of uneasiness touched me, for I saw that it was the man with the mask of Jock.

In the rocking and swaying and bumping, I was suddenly thrown against this costumed dancer, and I looked up into those light gray eyes. I knew those eyes and joy surged through me at the realization, leaving me weak and trembling. In the next instant he was gone, and I was flung away in Jean's arms, and he laughed as he kissed me.

The dancing began to pick up tempo and became quite frenzied; at last, when Jean and I stood aside panting for breath, I looked around for Danielle, but I couldn't see her right off. Only then did I dare look for the masked man, but I did not glimpse him again until much later.

We left the dancing then, and when Jean went to get us refreshments, I saw Danielle coming from the forest, her head down, and she seemed in a great hurry. Michel went to meet her and said something, but Danielle turned suddenly away from him and ran over to where Aimée was playing with some other children.

When Danielle looked around, she caught my eye, and I moved over to her. By this time she had somehow composed herself, and was smiling. "I was looking for you. I am going to take Aimée home now. No," she said as she waved a hand toward me, "you stay right here with Jean and enjoy the rest of the evening. I probably will come back. Papa . . . is going to drive me. If I don't return, the carriage will be sent back for you."

Jean hurried over to us and handed me the drink. "It's much worse than I thought. Labbé's men are causing the trouble," he said thickly.

"What happened?" Danielle asked in a queer voice.

"They're searching the mummers for spies against France." He was angry.

I was frightened now, and as I looked at Danielle, I saw her face had blanched. "But what do they mean? Why can't that man leave us alone? Oh, but I am going home, Jean. I . . . I don't want to watch this. . . ." She seemed quite upset.

Jean put his arm around his sister's shoulders. "Don't worry, Danielle. Maybe nothing at all will happen. But perhaps it's best if you go home."

By this time it was growing darker. Long shadows were falling, and we left Danielle waiting for the marquis to take her and Aimée to the carriage. Jean and I walked hand in hand through the old village.

"I saw the curé of our church earlier, and I mentioned that we wanted to talk with him. He didn't stay long at the festival, for he was called out to help one of the village people. But he said he'd be at the church at seven, and we could come then."

As we walked along over the cobblestones into the winding lanes, I vaguely noticed other couples around us, but I was deep in thought for a long while. I did not want to air my suspicions; indeed, I did not know what my suspicions were, nor did I know how Jean would react. I couldn't have mistaken those eyes, no. They belonged to my brother and I knew he was here and that he would be among those mummers searched by the police. If he were caught, might it not mean . . . death?

"You are strangely quiet, Tamar," Jean said in my ear, and I looked up at him. "You are disturbed. Tell me, what is bothering you, Tamar."

I swallowed and looked away. "I'm not hiding anything," I lied. I glanced around us. The village, one of those timeless ancient clusters of shops and houses, was much like those villages of our West Country in England. But because Jean was holding my hand, I was sure I had never seen a more colorful little village. I wished I could simply enjoy its beauty.

My voice was quiet. "When—when do you think my brother will come, Jean?"

His hand tightened on mine, pulling me closer

to his side as we strolled along. "You care a lot for him, don't you?"

"Yes. Of course. He is . . . my only family." My voice had a catch in it.

He was silent a moment, then said gently, "You will soon be a part of my family. Will that make you happy?" He stopped and turned me to face him, his hand warm on my neck. Passion flowed through me.

"I want Neville to share what I have, too, Jean. I want him to know my joy. Can you understand this? He was all I had all my life, you see." I remembered the look in Neville's eyes when he'd spoken of love and marriage that evening that seemed years ago instead of months ago. Yes. Neville had known love.

Jean rested his hands on my shoulders, looking at me. His eyes said everything I wanted to hear about our love for each other. It was only after we'd moved away and were at the cottage of the curé beside the old church that I realized he hadn't answered my question.

The curé, Pierre François, was tall and somewhere in his late thirties, I judged. He greeted Jean with warmth but I felt he was wary of me. I was not a Catholic, and I was sure he considered me a heretic.

"Won't you come in, Jean? I'm sure Mademoiselle Tamar and you are wanting to confer with me about something extremely important. We might as well make ourselves comfortable in my study." He smiled then, ironically, I thought, and I wondered how much this man of God knew about me. I knew he was not the same curé who had defended Jean's parents and this church, but he seemed to take on the responsibility of his parish with a zealousness of one dedicated.

We were led into the study and sat across from the priest. "Father, we want you to marry us. We would like it within the month, to be precise. Can you perform the ceremony?"

The curé looked startled, and for a brief moment I believe he was caught in surprise. "So you want to marry? And so soon." He lifted straight black brows. "You have talked this over with each other and are fully aware of what you both want? The sacrament of marriage is the exchange of vows between a man and a woman, and they are to be taken seriously." His eyes were like burning lumps of coal as they searched my face, seeing and knowing. He suddenly stood up and went to a tall cabinet in the corner, opened it and brought out a wine decanter and goblets.

Jean said, "Yes, we are both fully aware of this, Father François. . . ." He stopped as the sound of running footsteps came into the court, and a sudden pounding on the door interrupted him.

The curé, poised between the cabinet and table, lifted his eyes upward with a heavy sigh, then placed the decanter down and went to the door. "Yes? What is it?"

A young man stood there, breathless. "You must come, Father. There has been trouble. A man has been . . . killed."

Jean jumped up, holding my hand as the curé said, "What happened? Where?"

The young man, who had already started off at a run, called back, "At the festival grounds. You'd best hurry. The chief of police is asking for you." We followed, the curé carrying a black bag he'd grabbed on his way out the door.

An irrational wave of terror washed over me. The police had uncovered the mask and had discovered my brother! That was all I could think of. Dear God, I prayed, don't let it be Neville!

When we arrived, we saw a small crowd of men and women gathering in the trees. As we came closer, Jean suddenly held back, letting the curé hurry into the circle of people.

"Stay here, Tamar. Don't go any nearer. I will come back for you."

Even as he spoke, there was a break in the crowd and I could see it was not one of the mummers, for the man lying on the ground was not dressed in a costume. Jean left me and I watched as the curé reached the body and knelt, and Jean at his side, kneeling too. A tall black-clothed man stood staring down among the others there, but this man brought a chill shuddering through me. I guessed that he was the Monsieur Labbé of the police.

"He's dead," the curé said grimly, not looking up at the man standing over him. "Stabbed with a knife, it seems. Jean," he said, as he opened his bag and brought out a cross and placed it on the chest of the dead man, "where is your sister, Madame Danielle?"

"Mon Dieu!" I heard Jean exclaim, and I pushed through the crowd and rushed to his side, my throat tightening in pain. I stared, stunned,

for the man lying on the ground was Michel Cottereau.

"How did this happen? Why?" Jean asked incredulously, and I reached down to touch his shoulder, but he hardly knew I was beside him.

"There was a fight, a scuffle of sorts, with all the mummers about," said one of the men standing over the body. I thought I recognized him as one of the Cottereau family.

Jean glanced up to the man in black who was silent and watchful, intent upon Jean, the kneeling priest, and myself. He stood up. "What have you done, L'abbé, to set your henchmen on Michel Cottereau?" His face was dark with anger.

The accusation brought a dull flush to the man's face. "Who indeed would murder Citizen Cottereau, Monsieur de Rouvroy? Certainly not one of my men. Where were you when it happened?" His eyes raked over me, over Jean, and the priest. There was a silence, and the chief of police's gaze passed sinisterly over the crowd of people on the fringes, and on the group of mummers who I saw now were cordoned by several gendarmes. When those snake-like eyes touched my face again, I shivered and averted my own, staring down at the man who had been Danielle's husband, lying in a pool of blood on the ground.

Pierre François took a blanket from his bag and covered the body. I was hardly aware that Maurice and Charette had come running up to stand beside us, their faces shocked and pale as they learned the truth. Hardly anyone spoke.

Then the curé said, "I will go with him to the château, Monsieur de Rouvroy. Will you follow in the carriage? I think he should be placed in the wagon. Etienne here," he turned to Michel's relative, "will go tell the family." He took charge, summoning two gendarmes to lift the body and to carry it to the wagon.

Labbé spoke then. "Just one moment. I want a word with Monsieur de Rouvroy." He seemed furious that everything was being taken out of his hands.

Jean turned quickly, slapping his hand against his leg. "Why? I had nothing to do with this, as well you know, Labbé. Save your questions. I do not intend to subject myself or my family to your lurid persecutions." He was furious, and when he turned to me, I saw how taut his face was. He moved away quickly, and I hurried after him.

We settled ourselves in the carriage, Jean and I in back, and Maurice and Charette in the driver's seat. It was a silent ride back to the château, much different from the ride that had taken us to the field that morning. What had started out as a happy, carefree day had now ended in utter tragedy.

It was very late when at last we were able to go to our rooms; Danielle had been upset but she had not wept. The marquis too had been quite composed, and it was only when I excused myself and went to my rooms that I remembered seeing Danielle coming from those trees, Michel going to meet her, and her seemingly distraught state as she ran away from him.

Exhausted, I tried to sleep, but I could find no peace. I knew Neville had been behind that mask in that mummer's costume; I knew he was here, and my heart leaped with mixed emotions—joy and fear—for I knew the danger had now touched us all.

My mind was too active to find sleep. How would Neville get in touch with me? How would he let Jean know he was here? And just what lay ahead of us? I got up from the bed and began to pace the floor; I saw by the clock on the mantel that it was half-past three. It was colder, too, and I wrapped my robe about me, thinking of Neville and of the last time I'd seen him. I remembered the locket and went to get it, lighting the candle as I did so.

As I pulled it out from among my personal things, I thought of Neville and Danielle. When that "mummer" had danced with Danielle, had she been somehow aware, even after all this time? It occurred to me that she might have guessed, and that they . . . Could they have met in the forest?

My thoughts went crazy after that, my imagination stretching to guess what might have happened. They had met, and Neville had been angry that she was Michel's wife, and it was he who struck the fatal blow that would rid her of a husband, thus freeing Danielle. And why not? I thought bitterly. Was that why Danielle had been so composed when she'd learned of his death? Was that why she could shed no tears?

I told myself I was being ridiculous. Neville was not like that. I lifted the locket out to look at it once more, still full of questions, still wondering. . . .

Why else had Neville come? I was battling against jealousy with reason and logic, yet I knew it was not I whom Neville had come to search out, to speak with. He was most concerned with his one-time mistress, Danielle de Rouvroy!

But I was forgetting that Neville knew the entire situation with Jean, and therefore knew I would not be harmed. He could not yet know of our engagement, but he could be reasonably sure of Jean's motive for taking me away, and he was not worried.

I think I cried then, more out of anxiety than for the nightmare that the whole thing was spinning into. I returned to my bed after putting out the light, and lay there shivering, the locket still in my hands. I began to think I would never sleep, but eventually I fell into a rather troubled sleep, and it was quite late when I woke to find the household in a terrible state.

It was Charette who came to inform me I was wanted in the *grande salle*. I was astonished that she had the nerve to face me, but she seemed to have forgotten the unpleasantness between us. I was sipping my chocolate, already dressed to go find Aimée.

"The chief of police, Monsieur Labbé, is here. He wishes to speak with you." I had the impression that she was pleased.

"The chief of police? But why would he wish to see me?" I could hardly hide my astonishment.

"How should I know? Perhaps he has learned the truth about you." There was a look of malice in those bright black eyes that displeased and upset me.

"And just what *is* the truth, Charette?" I said icily, placing my cup down and standing to face her.

She shrugged her shoulders. "That you are not who Jean would have us believe you are, mademoiselle. I think you know what I'm talking about. You are the English spy's sister."

Incredulously I said, "And what English spy is that?" My own daring brought a sudden abashed expression to her eyes. "Wherever did you hear such a thing?" My voice was unnaturally high and tight with fear.

Again she shrugged. "That would be telling, wouldn't it? Make no mistake about it, mademoiselle," she said with a hiss. "Monsieur Labbé always learns the truth. He has been here for hours, asking questions. It will all come out, sooner than you think." With that, she turned and flounced out of my room.

I followed her out more slowly, apprehensive to say the least. As I walked along the corridors I wondered if it had not been Charette who had made Labbé suspicious of me. She hated me well enough, and because she had learned of Neville's existence from a source I was yet to discover, I was wary of her. Aside from that, I was dreading a talk with Labbé. To be questioned might mean that if the truth about Neville came out, it would go badly for me as well as for Jean, and Neville would be in grave danger.

Monsieur Labbé was in the *grande salle* with the marquis and Danielle, their contempt for this man more than obvious. I suspected that he felt uncomfortable, but he didn't let it show. The marquis came to my side, taking my hand in his. He seemed anxious.

"My dear Tamar," he said. "You will forgive us this once, won't you? It seems we are being forced into a rather ridiculous interrogation by the police. It has come to Labbé's knowledge that you are English, and thus you are under suspicion, even though our countries are at peace. Can you find it in your heart to bear this man's insufferable questions?" His eyes implored me to give nothing away, to say only what Jean had told everyone in the beginning.

I inclined my head, pressing my fingers on his hand, and saw that all he'd said had been intended for the ears of Monsieur Labbé. I believe the marquis was even conscious of his own imperious manner, that of a nobleman dealing with a most common servant. The man resented it, for as we walked toward him I could see it in every line of his face. But I went immediately to Danielle, taking her hand and kissing her cheek. Already she wore the black armband of mourning on her dark brown gown and her face was drawn and pale.

The marquis said evenly, "Mademoiselle Columb, may I present Monsieur Labbé, the chief of police at Brest. He is here to question us, I believe, about Monsieur Michel's death."

The man bowed politely, stiffly, affronted by the marquis's arrogance. "And when did you arrive in France, mademoiselle?" he asked without hesitation.

"It's been more than a fortnight now."

"From England?"

"No. From the . . . Straits, off the coast of Algiers."

He stared at me disbelievingly. "And what were you doing there?" he demanded. My heart nearly stopped at his blunt tactics, but the marquis came to my rescue.

"*Vraiment*, Monsieur Labbé, Mademoiselle Columb was on a ship captured by Barbary pirates. If it had not been for my son, she might now be in a sultan's harem."

Obviously, Monsieur Labbé did not like this interruption, and he might have gone on had Jean not stalked into the room. He came to my side at once.

"May I ask what right you have to subject my fiancée to this interrogation?"

"Your fiancée, Monsieur de Rouvroy? Ah, yes, I seem to recall now that there was mention of an engagement to this young woman. She is an English woman, *n'est-ce pas?*" It was said with the vilest of sneers, enraging even me, and I could see it took willpower for Jean to keep from striking out at the man. "It's my impression that it is a . . . sudden engagement, Monsieur de Rouvroy. Perhaps too sudden."

"We don't need your impressions, Labbé! As for all this, you are trespassing. I should be obliged if you would leave this house at once, as I know you've done all the questioning you came for. Michel Cottereau lies in one of our rooms. You have your suspects, now leave us."

"News came from Paris only yesterday that English agents are again filtering into the province, hoping to revive certain revolts against France

One is believed to be an Englishwoman, the sister of a notorious English spy who worked under the name Marc Renoire. I have the right to question this young woman, Monsieur de Rouvroy." His eyes lingered on Jean's face, then touched mine.

"What possible connection can there be between my fiancée and such a person as you describe? What could she know of this matter? You have already been told, no doubt, that I rescued Mademoiselle Columb from the hands of Barbary pirates, and she is not likely to be a British spy!"

Monsieur Labbé only raised speculative brows. He reached over to the table beside him and shuffled some papers uneasily. "But we shall see, Monsieur de Rouvroy. I have my investigations to attend to, and I will not relent until I learn the truth."

"You have no right to insinuate my fiancée is anything but who she is, Labbé! Now get out, before I have you thrown out!"

Labbé thrust the sheaf of papers into a leather case, unhurried by Jean's rage. He knows, I thought. And it was Charette who warned him.

"I will remind you I have not concluded my investigation. I will be back." His words were ominous, threatening, and he looked at me as if he could see my soul.

"Then conclude them elsewhere," remarked the marquis. "We are in mourning here, and we do not need reminders of your kind."

The man's black eyes were full of hatred. Obviously he was not satisfied, but he could do nothing about it, and he turned and left the room.

"Damned insolent man!" Jean exclaimed. I was shaken, and glancing at Danielle I saw her face was white and her eyes large and full of sorrow. But still she retained her pride and composure and sat through it all, saying nothing. But now she stood up and came over to me, putting her arm through mine.

"Tamar, let's go into the garden, shall we? I'm in need of fresh air. Jean, you won't mind if I take her for a while, will you?"

Jean seemed anxious, but he said, "I'll join you in a short time, if I may. I want to keep an eye on Labbé. I don't like having him around here."

"Nicolas is well out of the way, my boy," the marquis reassured him. "No need to concern yourself unduly. It was a senseless affair, all of it. I'm as puzzled as anyone that Michel should have been the victim of what Labbé is saying he is."

"And what is that?" Danielle said.

"That someone wanted to settle an old score with Michel. Heaven knows he's made plenty of enemies, switching camps as he did, but he was not an informer. That much I know. There's talk that the person who did it was costumed just like the others and therefore got away, slipping away in that crowd. It's most unfortunate, though, to have it happen now. We didn't need to be put in the limelight for the chief of police to come probing around. Everything will be called off, for the time being."

Jean's face was an unreadable mask, and Danielle was not objecting. My heart fluttered. Oh, dear God, I prayed silently, don't let it be Neville.

He couldn't—he wouldn't murder a man in cold blood!

"I shall be riding down to where *L'Angélique* is anchored this afternoon," he said carefully. "Will you ride with me, Tamar?"

"Of course," I said anxiously. I had a feeling that Jean had a special reason for asking me to accompany him. Perhaps he was planning to hide me from Labbé. But something in the back of my mind told me Neville was involved. Could Jean have been in contact with him?

As Danielle and I left the *grande salle,* Maurice hurried through, taking only enough time to touch Danielle's cheek with affectionate sympathy. "Don't grieve over what is done, cousin," he said in a surprising rush of tenderness. "I think Monsieur Labbé will discover the villain who did this, and justice will be carried out."

"An eye for an eye, Maurice? Is that what you call justice?" She eyed him impatiently, but with cool reserve, and the young man's face flushed at this reproach. "It seems you have faith in Monsieur Labbé!" He squared his jaw.

"He was your husband, Danielle. Surely you wish his murder avenged? I can assure you that all of this is becoming a great threat to the offenders to the New Order, this tallying up old scores of the Royalists' days."

"And how is it becoming a threat?" Danielle asked softly. She never once forgot her station in life, I thought.

"It's bringing the old offenders into the lime-light, separating them from the rest who went along with the justice for the people's cause.

181

Michel Cottereau, brother to one of the most notorious leaders of the Royalists in Brittany. Who wouldn't want to even the score with him and his kind?" There was a fire-bright look in his eyes, and he reached out and took her hand, bringing it to his lips.

"Don't look so angry. I'm sorry. I shouldn't have reminded you of the past. I was always puzzled about why Uncle Honoré and Aunt Louisa allowed you to return to fight with the Resistance. It must have been terrible for them to know you were in such danger all that time." For a moment I believed she was ready to strike him, but she did not. She turned to me.

"We were headed for the garden, were we not, Tamar dear?" The young man smiled, bowed slightly to us both, and he turned and left us. Danielle led the way out of the house into the court. The air was pungent, biting with an early frost, and I was glad of the woolen gown I wore now.

"When Sister Magdaleine came from the convent earlier this morning, she asked to take Aimée back with her for a few hours. I knew that she might be upset about what has happened, and of course I wanted to spare her some of the sordid facts of life for the moment. She will have time enough for learning all that sorrow. Can you understand that, Tamar?"

"Yes," I agreed quietly. "She and Michel were not close. But she will have to be told. She will have to know of his death."

"Yes. Oh, yes. But I will tell her gently—when I'm calmer myself." She sighed, but I could see an excitement in her eyes. I followed her gaze as it moved from my face into the garden. Her face was pink and a secretive smile curved her lips. No, she was not a grieving widow, yet—

"Tamar." Her voice was quite low and soft. "I didn't know . . . I never suspected it, but you are . . . Marc's sister, aren't you?"

My heart drummed a frantic beat. "I don't know this Marc Renoire," I said. "I've only heard that name since I've been here."

She stared at me, those dark eyes full of wonder, yet of puzzlement. "You must be. For now I know the truth about your coming here, and how it is involved with what Jean, the marquis, and Nicolas are planning. It was all a cover, and I know it, Tamar." She looked at me with this knowledge, and although I knew I could not hide it from her, I averted my eyes and said nothing. She had guessed, then, and perhaps that is how Charette came to know it—perhaps she had guessed the truth as well.

We were silent for a short time, then I said, "You . . . know this man, Marc Renoire?"

"Yes. I . . . know him," she said quietly. But something in her voice made me turn and stare at her. It held that special note of joy that could no longer be kept a secret. "I loved him—we loved each other deeply. And I was . . . fortunate."

"He is Aimée's father? This Englishman?"

Her eyes turned on me, glowing. "Yes. Marc is my daughter's father."

"Yet you married Michel Cottereau but six months ago."

She seemed to flinch at the mention of his

name. "I did not love Michel, that is true. But I believed Marc was dead, or I shouldn't have ever been Michel's wife."

"And now?"

"Now I know I was wrong. Marc is alive. I . . . I know he is here in Brittany. Yesterday—" She stopped, seeing my expression. My heart thudded inside me, hammering until my ears roared. I was seeing yesterday: Neville. The masked mummer she danced with, and met in the forest.

It was all too clear. She had been seen by Michel. There were angry words, and then Michel was murdered by one of those masked mummers.

Now the way was paved for Michel's widow and Marc Renoire! I was afraid now, desperately afraid.

She began talking. "Tamar, I had no idea Marc was alive until yesterday. But even had there not been proof yesterday, I should have known it today."

"What happened yesterday?" My throat was tightening with that fear.

"Marc was there, dancing in the costume of a mummer. I could not fail to know him. It left me breathless. Can you understand? I believed him dead. All those years—those long months after Quiberon, I was in a semi-daze. Marc, my love, as well as my mother and father, brutally murdered because of a senseless betrayal, all three gone from my life. I wanted to die too, you see. But there was Marc's child. He did not get my message. He thought I'd been killed too that night. How ironic! I waited. I was sure he'd received my message, but now I know he did not."

The message tucked behind the picture of Danielle inside the locket—the locket which I now had inside my pocket. I could barely speak.

"What happened? I mean, you sent a message . . ." My words seemed hollow.

She looked away into the garden, and it was as if she slipped back into that time, forgetting me. "Marc came to us when my parents and I slipped back into France during the Resistance. You can't imagine how it was then, Tamar. We were all fugitives, not known at the château, and my parents were not the Marquis and Marquise de Rouvroy. We went under assumed names, all of us. Even Marc, so I did not know his English name, but he knew ours from the beginning. It was like that, you see, because of his government contacts." She smiled. "He was tall, very English, yet he spoke French as though he were indeed French. I fell in love with him the first morning we met, going into the caves. His eyes were the color of sea and cloud in a coming storm, and there could be no mistake about how we felt. We both knew it, that we were meant for each other."

How could I not know what she was talking about, when my own love was like this? I could not hold it against her. She went on.

"For a long time I did not let my parents know about us. We kept it secret, and that was easy to do, for they moved quickly from place to place, running the ambush lines near Nantes, my mother right beside my father. She was a courageous woman, and my father was fortunate in having her with him, believing what he believed in. I think they would have understood, had I let them know about Marc. He wanted to tell them, but I was the one who held back. The curé knew, for he married us."

"You were *married*? To Marc?" The astonishment was clear in my voice.

She didn't mind, it seemed. "Oh, yes. It had to be that way with Marc. We had the blessing of the church, a secret simple ceremony with our vows spoken. Aimée is not illegitimate, Tamar."

I was silent for a moment, and then I said, "Does no one else know you were married to . . . Marc?"

She shook her head. "No. I didn't see any reason to . . . confess it to anyone afterward. Why should I have told them? Marc was dead. All meaning was gone. I left it at that."

I could offer nothing to say except, "What happened after you were married?"

"Marc and I remained in the caves at our headquarters, for Marc was running things behind the scenes. We had six months of loving each other, of living in a joy that nothing could touch. He often talked of taking me to Cornwall with him. He would say over and over, 'My home is nothing like the Château de Rouvroy, mind you, but it's beautiful. I want to take you there, when all this is over. After Quiberon. I want us to leave here so that my children are born in peace.'

"And of course I believed that was how it would be. We planned, you see. Our happiness left us both in a golden trance, for we did not see the possibility that it could all fail—those plans, so carefully and secretly drawn up to break through General Hoche's tight cordon around the coast.

That landing of the troops at Quiberon was supposed to overcome our enemy, and then we would march to Paris to restore the Bourbon king in his rightful place." She spoke with a trace of bitterness that reflected all the suffering she went through for that cause.

"You had great faith in what you believed in," I said.

"Yes. We all had faith, except for the . . . betrayer. There's one in every camp, they say. But how should we have known him? The *Chouans* were closely knit. The Cottereau family were our fiercest believers in the cause, loyal and staunch. I still believe it would have gone well, at least most of our people would have escaped to safety, if there had not been a betrayal. Betrayals were common enough in the Revolution, it's true, but not among the *Chouans*. It was the first one, and the last. And it cost us the lives of our faithful . . . leaders, as well as the cause itself."

"You must have suffered . . . much."

She only bowed her head, remembering. "Others suffered too. It was our lot."

"Will you tell me about it?"

"Naturally, General Hoche's own spy system was working too—counterspies and the lot. They knew there would be a massive landing, but they couldn't know what date. My Uncle Henri, my father's twin brother, came in the weeks prior to the landing. You may or may not be aware of this, Tamar, but the marquis is not . . . our father, Jean's and mine." Her voice lowered to a whisper.

I met her eyes and said simply, "Jean told me."

"I suspected that he would tell you. Truth is always best, or else we find ourselves in tangled webs too often. Uncle Henri is living out this lie, but he feels that he is trying to make amends for what went wrong. In a way I think he blames himself."

"I understood that he had remained in exile in England."

She smiled. "Uncle Henri was one of the key people in England who kept supply routes open for the Resistance. My father and Uncle Henri could have exchanged places with each other at any time if they chose, for they were that much alike. It was hard to believe that he was not my father, when all of it was over. But he came to Brittany, and brought with him another English agent whose name I only knew as André. Uncle arrived unexpectedly, in spite of the danger, and came to the caves with André. Then my parents came with Josef Cottereau, Nicolas's father, and Michel's brother. There were several other leaders there, including the curé of our church. And, of course, the big campaign was plotted as to how to cut through Hoche's watch, and even take him captive if necessary."

We were strolling through the gardens now, and she stooped down and plucked a marigold, breathing in its fragrance.

"The betrayer had to have been with us at that time, Tamar. No other people knew those plans."

"And he has not been caught?"

She shook her head. "No. Not to my knowledge. He went free, I suppose. But nature played her part too, in that drama, for a heavy fog blanketed the coast—so thick that hardly anything could move. Why even during the day it was impossible to get out on the water in our boats to give signals. We didn't dare give the signals on land, but had to go out into the water and approach our ships coming in. Marc was in charge of an ambush scheme right on Quiberon Bay, and my parents were to hold another similar ambush inland, with Josef Cottereau and his men to aid them. Afterward they would be led to our hideouts. I was going to remain in the caves that week. Marc insisted, and I would have done so had it not been for Uncle Henri."

There was unmeasurable sadness in her voice. "Uncle Henri became worried after Marc and my parents left. The fog had worsened, and on the night before the scheduled landing he asked if I would go with several other young women, as I had done this many times before, to that enemy camp to entice the officers to drink heavily, and to drug their drinks with sedatives. I agreed, and we set out immediately.

"But when I reached those lines, I turned to Uncle Henri and asked if he would give a message to Marc for me. He was going to steal into Marc's company, and he agreed to give Marc my note, which was tucked inside a locket."

"Je ne doutes pas que vous vendriez." The words slipped from my mouth. "I do not doubt that you will come!" My voice was a whisper.

She shot around. "Where did you hear that?"

"I saw it in the locket. I have it with me." I brought out the locket and gave it to her.

"Where did you find this?" Her expression was one of shocked disbelief.

"I discovered it at Columb Manor."

"So he *did* have it." Her voice was faint, and her face paled.

I shook my head. "Neville—my brother—did not recognize it. I found it, you see, out in the gardens. Neville commented on its rare beauty, but he did not know it. He thought it must have belonged to my mother."

"Then how could it have been in Cornwall?" she asked, mystified.

"I cannot know this. Did your uncle say that Marc had it?"

She nodded. "Of course, I did not see Uncle Henri for many months after that night. In fact it was almost two years before he slipped into France again. He had escaped with his life that night, but he didn't know what had happened to Marc. Naturally he didn't guess that I was Marc's wife and, well, he believed as others did, after my child was born, that her unknown father was dead. I didn't speak of it to him."

She looked so unbearably stricken that my eyes misted over with tears; then she went on. "Everything was so blindingly sudden and quick that night. You've heard how vengeance can swoop down on the unsuspecting? Well, it was so. We were caught, those other girls and I, caught with the drugs. That is why I knew there had to have been a betrayal. Those officers waited for us to make our overtures before exposing us, and for our punishment we were used in a most vile manner. I know Marc would never have left me to such a fate had he known.

"Then we were imprisoned, but I was released

after three days, and how I got back I shall never know. I learned of my parents' deaths, the deaths of *everyone* loyal it seemed, but I came back to hide in the caves, and the Cottereau family aided me. I shan't ever forget their care of me; even in the midst of their own peril, they helped me. Then Jean came home. He was with me when my daughter was born."

I could not fathom her suffering in those horrors. My heart cried for her, and I knew exactly why Jean so desperately wanted vengeance.

For a time she was silent, deep in her own past. She knew Marc was here. She had seen him and had talked with him; her love was still with him. But my fears quickened.

"Did Michel know . . . Marc?" I could hardly get the words out.

She glanced up at me, troubled, then looked away. "Yes. They had to know each other. Michel knew of . . . my attachment to him, and he was jealous, although I had never even looked at Michel. Not even during that time when his family looked after me. Nor would I have ever considered marriage with him, had I known Marc was alive. That made our marriage—the one to Michel—not a marriage at all, for I was a married woman—I am Marc's wife. In a way it makes all this easier to bear." She meant, I knew, Michel's death.

"I marvel that you could have married him."

"It was for monetary reasons, so Uncle Henri kept pointing out to me. The Cottereau family thrived in their business, and Michel ran the Farms with perfected skill. It was not easy, but because I married Michel, a great debt on the château was paid in full. We owed the Cottereau family much for saving our home." She was humbled, but proud.

"You are a courageous woman, Danielle," I murmured, meaning it, my eyes moist.

She turned to me and clutched my arm. "Listen to me, Tamar," she said, her eyes bright. "You must promise me that you will make Jean see how useless this cause for the Bourbon revival in France is. He is unsure, I know. But I am certain it will all lead to disaster. Because I know that Napoléon Bonaparte will not suffer the Resistance again. He will win. Make Jean know that, Tamar. He loves you. He can be persuaded. I know."

I doubted that, but I faced her with hope in my heart as I said that I could try. We could not continue our conversation, for one of the servants came running to say that guests had arrived to pay their respects. But Danielle whispered to me as she turned to follow the servant in, "I do not believe that Marc had any part in this crime, Tamar. You cannot believe it either. We may never know who betrayed us, but I know in my heart that it was not Marc!"

7

I went immediately to my rooms to think over all that Danielle had told me. I was more than disquieted that Neville was here in Brittany somewhere, as much as I had suspected it before, hiding perhaps in those caves at this very moment. I wondered again why he hadn't tried to contact me in any way.

Danielle had said that her Uncle Henri had given the locket with its message to Marc. And he knew that Marc was Neville Columb, for how else could Jean have come to Columb Manor for me? And the locket had been there for me to discover.

I was restless. I paced the floor, sorting out all the unmatched pieces of the puzzle. What was it Jean had said of his Uncle Henri? I tried to recall the words he spoke that afternoon in the cabin of *L'Angélique*. Henri de Rouvroy had told Jean the whole story, had said that it was Marc Renoire who'd betrayed his parents that night and had left

Danielle to her fate at the mercy of those men.

If all this were true, then Neville had lied to me about not ever having seen that locket. I wouldn't believe that of my brother. Why should he have denied seeing it? And Danielle said that he'd never received the message. But how did the locket come to be in the bush where I found it? If Neville had not dropped it there, who else could have done so?

Danielle did not believe that Marc was capable of betrayal, nor of the coldblooded murder of Michel Cottereau. And I could not believe it of my brother either. A cold fear possessed me then, and the uneasiness stayed with me even when I joined the family for our luncheon. What seemed so strange was that Michel's presence at the table was not missed. For the first time, I studied the marquis's face, thinking that the resemblance to Jean was that of father and son. Not even Maurice looked as much like the marquis, and he was his son.

The dark eyes, like Jean's, glanced around the table thoughtfully and came to mine, resting briefly, with just a trace of a smile, as if he knew I was silently questioning his double role in this household.

No mention was made of the man lying in one of the other rooms; it was as if they had concluded the man's existence in their lives, and were now concerned only with outwitting the contemptible chief of police.

Charette's attitude gave me an uncomfortable feeling too; her eyes watched me closely and then studied Jean. Because of her dislike of me, I suspected it was she who had talked with Monsieur Labbé. And it seemed to me that she had learned something, for her expression gave every indication that she knew far more of what was going on than those at the table knew she did.

The marquis said, "Have you two lovebirds decided to go on with your plans of an early marriage, Jean? In spite of . . ." he gestured with his hands, and a shrug of his shoulders, ". . . all this?" The brown eyes were sincere and warm as he looked at me, with affection, I thought.

"Yes. I see no reason not to," Jean said, "and I'm sure Danielle will agree." He eyed his sister.

Danielle shook her head and answered, "I have no objections, Jean. We can be a little discreet in the celebrations, and if it is a quiet affair, then I see no reason to wait."

Maurice laughed. "I dare say I would not give it a second thought if Mademoiselle Tamar were to be my bride either! As it is I have had to give second and third thoughts already, and as you see, have not had the courage to leap."

"That's because you haven't met the right one, Maurice," Danielle said wisely. "Tamar is good for Jean. They will make a good life for each other."

I looked at Charette, expecting a protest, but except for a tiny gleam of dislike for me in her eyes, she had no comment to make. I could only suppose that Maurice's presence kept her in line. Danielle had been sure that he would bring her to her senses where Jean was concerned, and it appeared that he had been at least moderately successful.

"You seem so sure, cousin," Maurice said, his eyes on me, flattering me with his glance. "I believe Mademoiselle Tamar would be good for me too, if I were in Jean's place. You are fortunate, Jean."

"I know I am."

"We are all fortunate that she is to be part of our family." The marquis lifted his glass of wine, and we all drank, except Charette. She stood up then and asked if she could be excused, and without waiting, she left the room.

Maurice stared after her. "*Mon Dieu,* but she has it bad, *n'est-ce pas?*" He drained his glass and stood up. "I will go talk with her. Hot-headed little minx that she is, she just might do something drastic. Will you excuse me, uncle?" He was so polite that I marveled at his sister's lack of discipline.

The marquis nodded his head. "See if you can talk some sense into her, my boy. She is beyond me at the moment, I fear."

"That I will attempt." He nodded to Danielle and to me, then with a mock salute to Jean, he left us, hurrying after his sister.

We were silent for a moment, all of us lost in thought about Charette and her obsession for Jean. Then Jean explained we had a long ride ahead of us, and that we'd best be going, so we left Danielle and the marquis. Glad of the escape, I hurried to my rooms to change into my riding habit, but I could not rid my thoughts of the growing fear that Charette had been the one who had warned the chief of police.

A short time later I made my way down to the stables in the courtyard. I didn't see Jean, so I went inside, the smell of hay and pitch strong in my nostrils, a scent that took me back to Columb Manor and our one small stable. These stables were huge. I wandered inside and began to amble down through the stalls to see the beautiful creatures munching contentedly from their feed buckets.

There was no one about, and although I knew Jean would come at any moment, I lingered there, admiring the beautiful animals with their long silky necks. I couldn't have been in there more than a few minutes, but in that time I became conscious of several figures, at least three, standing vigil in the shadows. It shocked me, although I should have been prepared for it, and I knew then that Monsieur Labbé had his men posted to watch every move we made.

I turned to walk quickly from the stables and out into the sun, in time to see Jean striding across the courtyard, his face a dark study. I ran to him, still frightened.

"Jean. They are . . . in there. Men posted about. Does Monsieur Labbé have the right to do this?"

"Yes, damn him! Labbé is taking no chances. I don't think they will be here long, but their presence has already had an effect on everyone, even the servants." He took my arm. "Don't be frightened. Those men will do no harm here; and everything is safe. Don't worry."

"I can't help it." I bit my lip to keep from mentioning my brother's name, and telling him of my fears. I was afraid we would be overheard, even here.

"Come on. Let's take our mounts and ride out. We can speak of these things later, and I want to make sure all is well with *L'Angélique*. Just don't be afraid." He smiled down at me, making me forget my fears for the moment.

"Very well," I said. We walked arm in arm across the stableyard where our saddled mounts awaited us. In less than five minutes we were out of the gates and riding toward the cliffs, with the cool sea wind in our faces. We rode along for some time without speaking.

The sky was pale blue, the churning water icy green as it crashed against the rocks, and the gulls' forlorn cries were distant as they soared up on the wind and sailed downward again. We stopped and looked over the cliff's edge, side by side.

"We shall have rain and very soon," Jean said, looking up at the sky. "Our fine weather will go, and it will be cold." Then he smiled at me, his eyes shining. "I spoke with Pierre François this morning, Tamar. We can be married sooner than we expected. You won't mind a quiet wedding, will you?"

It took my breath away for an instant, so intense was my joy. "It seems a . . . beautiful way to be married," I said. "When will it be?"

"As soon as the final arrangements are made. Within the week."

My heart skipped a beat, for more than anything I wanted what Jean wanted, to be married within the church. But I wanted to talk with my brother first, I wanted Neville to share in my happiness. Yet I was reluctant to talk to Jean about it. I wondered if he still hated Neville as he once had.

Jean spurred his horse ahead and I followed. We came at last to the cove where *L'Angélique* rocked on her moorings, and the rocks out in the shimmering bay rose in pink shadows, with flocks of gulls like shredded paper around them. The ship was handsomely built, with long slim lines, and as we paused to look at her, I understood the pride Jean felt. I saw the look of pleasure touch his face, and for a moment we said nothing. When I glanced at the ship again, I could see men on her deck, and guessed that they were anxious to see their captain again.

We moved down into the dense trees, and when we reached them, the sudden screech call pierced the afternoon, shocking me so that I jerked around. Jean reached over and touched my arm in reassurance.

"The *Chouan* call for all is clear," Jean explained, seeing my fright. "It's safe here. I believe Monsieur Labbé is afraid to probe too deeply. There are too many who want personal revenge."

We dismounted and while he tethered our horses in the trees, I looked around me, recalling that night I had first seen this place, and a sense of time and distance touched me then—how far I had traveled since that night!

We walked down to the small stone quay where the sailor I recognized from that first night awaited us. Jean greeted him as Pierre, and the swarthy man grinned from ear to ear. They spoke for a moment in low tones, and then I was helped down into the boat.

We were rowed out to the waiting ship, the wind on my face. I could sense Jean's mounting excitement; I remembered Danielle's pleading request of me, imploring me to make her brother give up this lost cause. I was not sure that she was right, for Jean loved France, and I recalled that my own brother had believed in it too. These thoughts passed through my mind during that short ride across the bay, as we approached *L'Angélique.*

I followed Jean up the ladder and felt his hands help me onto the deck; I looked down into the grinning face of Jock who waited there for his master. There seemed to be a bit of commotion aboard, a current of excitement coursing through the men themselves, but Jean hurried me down the steps into the galleyway and to the cabin I recalled with vivid memory.

Jean opened the door and stepped aside to allow me to enter. And there stood Neville beside the window, in rough leather breeches and coarse linen shirt. He was handsome, his eyes alive with light, and alert on my face.

I forgot everything as he moved toward me and I ran into his arms, bursting into tears of relief and joy.

After a long moment with his arms about me he put me back from him and said, "Now why the tears? I thought you'd be glad to see me, kitten." He smiled in the old tender way and handed me his handkerchief.

"I am. Oh, I am, but it's so wonderful—such a

relief to know you are here. Oh, Neville! I have so much to tell you—so much has happened—"

"I know, I know," he said with tenderness, as he led me to the chairs at the table; he stood beside me, affectionate and every bit as wonderful as I remembered him to be. I suddenly became aware that Jean had left us, closing the door softly, and I now felt a pang of regret that I hadn't included him.

I said, "How on earth did you get here?"

He lifted an eyebrow, standing back and then sitting on the edge of the table, holding one of my hands in his. "You mean on this ship? It was arranged by those who abducted you to bring me here to Brittany to organize the *Chouan* movement again. Have they treated you all right, Tamar?"

"Oh, yes." I wanted him to know about Jean. But I said instead, "How did you get to Brittany? When?"

"Actually it was Cameron who suggested we take a ship out of Penzance bound for Portugal, and we worked our way through the borders."

"Cameron!" I stared at him.

"Yes, of course. Don't you know he would not allow his betrothed to remain for long in the clutches of her abductor?" He laughed.

"You don't mean he's . . . here?" I asked.

"Well, yes, he's here in Brittany. So you are safe, my dear. But may I add that you don't look as if you were ever a prisoner of some devil of a Frenchman! In fact, I'd say you had the look of a woman in love, for I've not seen you look all starry-eyed . . ." He raised my hand to his lips, his eyes penetrating mine.

"Does it show?"

"To me it shows. So confess. Even yesterday while you were dancing, there was no mistaking that look."

"Then it *was* you behind the mask!"

"Yes, it was. Come on now, tell me what has happened to make you look like that?"

"Yes. I am in love, and with Jean de Rouvroy."

He whistled. "You and Jean. What about Cameron?"

"Oh, Neville. He doesn't . . . exist any more for me. He never really did, you know. Jean and I— we're going to be married."

"Are you sure?" But he smiled. "Of course you're sure. I see it in your eyes, and you're happy."

"Deliriously so!" I cried.

"Then I'm glad. I suppose I'm invited to the wedding?"

"It couldn't go on without you. I am glad you're here, Neville." I inclined my head to one side. "You are . . . Marc Renoire, aren't you?"

"How did you know?"

"You are Danielle's husband then." My voice was quiet.

I saw by his face that my knowledge of this shocked him. "Danielle told me this morning. Why didn't you ever tell me, Neville?"

He stared at me for a long moment. Then he stood up and walked over to stare out the window. "I couldn't. I believed she was dead. Useless, wasted. . . ." He stopped, then finished, "All of it was over for me then, and I made up my mind I would bury all of it. I couldn't speak of it, not even to you."

I believed I could understand. "You thought she was dead? Is that when you escaped?"

He turned back to me. "I had no idea that she had gone with those girls to the officers' camp. I would never have agreed to that. Everything failed that night, and our losses were great, but I managed to escape and went back to the caves where I thought she would be waiting. As soon as I got there, word came that her parents and Josef and the curé had been shot and that she was with them. I was also told that I was being hunted. I left the caves and made my escape by rowing out to an English ship that night."

"You never received her message—Danielle's?"

He shook his head. "She told me of it only yesterday."

"Did you not see Henri de Rouvroy during that night? It was he who carried the message."

He was silent. "I know there was betrayal that night. But it was not Henri de Rouvroy."

"Neville. You didn't recognize that locket she placed the message in. Yet it was there at Columb Manor. I discovered it that day you came back from London, remember? And you didn't know it. I had already found the message there, behind a picture of Danielle."

He watched me for a moment. "And you believed I brought it there?"

I shook my head. "Not now. But someone betrayed you as well as the others. I know that. And Jean believes it was you. He believes that you left

Danielle at the mercy of those men that night."

"I suspected as much when he had me knocked over the head and took you with him," he chuckled. "But I think he knows more of the truth now. We have straightened out a few things between us."

"But his uncle told him that it was you, Marc Renoire, who betrayed them that night! It drove him to Columb Manor to abduct me and to get his revenge."

There was genuine surprise in his expression as he said, "Henri told him that?" He was silent for a moment. "Now that is something I didn't know. I don't believe anyone knows who betrayed us, not yet. But it may come out sooner than we think."

I was suddenly afraid for him. "Monsieur Labbé questioned me today, Neville. You know about Michel Cottereau's death?"

He nodded. "Yes. But why did the chief of police question you?" He was alert.

"Someone must have informed him I was the sister of Marc Renoire. What's more, he knows somehow that you're back in Brittany."

"Damn! Then he probably thinks it is I who stabbed Michel Cottereau, if I know Labbé! He'll make some excuse to hound me for his own sweet revenge. But we are safe enough. We shall just lie low and organize on the quiet. This wedding of yours—how soon is it to take place?"

"Within the week. It is to be a quiet affair, because of . . ."

"Yes, I know. The house is in mourning." He came to me and pulled me to him. "You are very lucky indeed, Tamar. Very lucky to have a young man like Jean de Rouvroy." He held me close, and I was thankful that he understood my feelings.

"Now, an unforeseen blessing lies in this wedding. It could be the very cover we need to get the scent off our trail. You have my blessing, Tamar."

"I've been so afraid for you, Neville."

"You mustn't be. But to tell the truth, until I actually arrived, I was quite worried about you. I hadn't a notion of who Jean de Rouvroy was, not until that last moment, and by then it was too late. Afterward I knew it was all a ruse to get me back into action again."

I stood back from him. "Who did kill Michel, Neville?"

He stared at me. "Good God, you didn't think I did?" How perceptive he was, I suddenly thought, and reddened.

"It . . . entered my mind, yes. He was Danielle's husband."

"No, never that! I was her husband, all this time. I *am* her husband." He was defiant, a dark resentment rising toward the man who'd taken his wife.

"You love her, don't you, Neville?"

"I fell in love with Danielle the moment I saw her, Tamar. There's been no other woman for me, and I would have done anything to get her out of France. If I had known that she'd been . . . alive, I would have moved heaven and earth to get to her. Now I have come to take my wife—and my daughter—home with me."

"You have seen Aimée?"

"From a distance." I heard a wistful note in his voice, and suddenly remembered how the masked man had stood on the fringe of the crowd watching another mummer entertain and delight the little girl who was his daughter.

"I can guess. And I've been her 'governess,' " I laughed, "teaching her English, mind you."

"Good girl. She is going to need it. She's a pretty child, isn't she?" I couldn't mistake the pride in his voice.

"She's all that and more, Neville dear. Because you are her father, because she is Danielle's and yours. From your love." My own heart was full in that moment, and my eyes filled with tears again.

"You are not sorry, are you, kitten?"

I shook my head, smiling through the tears. "No, oh no. I'm glad you have a family! So very glad, Neville!"

So it was a moment of closeness between my brother and me, and I knew I had grown up and away from that possessiveness.

"We are all a family, my dear. And you have your own love now. But—" He stepped back and looked teasingly serious. "What are we going to do about Cameron? He must be told. And his family is waiting and worrying over your fate with the Frenchman, I might add. Cameron was angry, and wanted to rush after that ship and rescue you, challenging the Frenchman to a duel. I had to restrain him. But you'll have a hard time trying to convince him that Jean did not forcibly seduce you, my dear sister."

Blushing deeply, I met his eyes. "Then we shall tell him, Jean and I. You don't mind about all that, do you? I mean, that it's not Cameron, but Jean?"

"Good God, no! I'm happy for you, because you are a woman in love, and I am proud of you and of the man who is responsible for it."

"Thank you," I said huskily, blinking back tears. "I hoped you would be."

"What a twist of fate . . . your Jean being Danielle's brother! It's strange, don't you think?" But his eyes were shining, and I remembered with a pang how I'd been jealous. "Jean and . . . you." He spoke slowly, a kind of wonderment in his expression.

"Very strange indeed. Oh, Neville," I said suddenly, "Danielle wants me to persuade Jean to leave this cause. That he didn't get a chance to be with the Resistance in those days rests heavily on his conscience. She doesn't want to see him running like a fugitive, for she believes that Bonaparte will not lose. She fears for him."

He became quiet, crossing his arms over his chest. "But he will not, is that it? If what I know about this young gallant is true, he won't easily be persuaded. It's all so very touchy. Go carefully, Tamar. But hadn't we best have him join us now? It's time I had a talk with your fiancé, I believe."

He crossed the room and opened the door, then called out something in rapid French, and in a very few moments Jock appeared with some hot coffee and Jean came in behind him. I knew instantly that it was he who had arranged this meeting, and that because he knew of the closeness between Neville and me he had seen to it that my brother would be there at the exchange of our vows. It moved me to a joy that brought tears close as he took my hand and smiled down at me before we faced Neville.

The two men faced each other, then shook hands, and Neville said, "So you want to ask for the hand of my sister, Jean?" How serious he was.

"Yes. I believe Tamar would like your presence at the wedding. It would please me also if you were there."

"Then it is settled. Tamar tells me it will take place within the week. I'm sure you'll arrange all the necessary precautions."

"Of course. But we must not take any more risks than necessary. We must return to the château now, Tamar, and Pierre will see you back to the caves as you came, Neville." They were on first name basis, and in my astonishment at this a true sense of relief flooded through me. Perhaps Jean had realized that my brother could not have betrayed anyone, least of all the woman he loved and her parents. I realized that Jean and Neville must have had prior contact, maybe sometime on the feast day.

"Quite so. Let's be quick. Send the message by the usual route, and I'll be there. By the way," he said as he took a long swallow of the hot sweet coffee, "I understand you are required to make a show at the reception the first consul has ordered at the Tuileries. Quite an affair, I presume. I suggest you go and make an impression, Jean. Nothing could relieve the little general more than to have certain subjects appear loyal to him." There was a dry, sarcastic note in his voice, and Jean agreed.

"I intend to take Tamar with me, as my wife."

Neville raised his brows, looking from Jean to me. "Be careful. Never trust anyone in those circles. They say the wine flows and the jewels sparkle, and Bonaparte flaunts himself throughout. He would be made emperor of the French, and, by God, he just may be able to convince France that is what they want!"

"I will take care of Tamar," Jean said gravely. "Maurice, my cousin, will be riding in with us. He has won favor in *mon général*'s eyes. I doubt if Uncle Henri will attend now, because of the death of my sister's husband. The family will be in mourning."

"Properly so," Neville said dryly. "We want no suspicions cast upon the Château de Rouvroy. We shall outwit the chief of police, if we can maintain a proper front."

In the small silence which followed this thought, it came to me that Jean did not know my brother was Danielle's husband; he would be thinking of Neville as her old lover. But I knew it was for either Neville or Danielle to enlighten Jean, and not myself; their secret had been well kept for all these years, and until they decided they wanted it known, it would remain their secret.

After a moment Jean said, "We'd best be on our way. Wait inside until the signal is given. We did have men watching us as we left the château, and they could have followed us. Labbé does not trust us an inch."

"Nor should he," Neville laughed. He looked at

me. "Go carefully, my dear. Let Jean look after you. Trust no one else."

"Neville," I said, touching his arm. "Please do not run risks. I will see to everything—" I didn't finish, but I could see that he knew I meant I would look after his daughter for him.

"I take the least risks possible, Tamar. You will learn this. Now go with Jean." I put my arms around his neck and kissed his cheek, and he touched mine. Jean had already gone through the door and held it open for me, and the two men saluted silently.

We hurried into the waiting boat, and it was only when we fetched our horses and were riding back to the château that I remembered that I hadn't even asked where in Brittany Cameron Pennland was, and I wondered just how soon it would be before I had to face him and tell him of Jean. But even that thought was fleeting, for I was content to be in the company of my love, and I quickly forgot about Cameron.

The long night's vigil before the day of the funeral for Michel began the next evening, and while members of the Cottereau family filed in to keep their half-hour watch, I went with Danielle to the church where the curé had taken the body. But even there, there was a sense of brooding danger and menace because of the presence of the chief of police and his men posted to look into the faces of every member of the family in the search for Nicolas.

On the day of the funeral I remained at home with Aimée, for she'd been unduly upset when she'd somehow discovered that her stepfather had been lying asleep in the back parlor. But it was Charette who had told her that Michel was dead, stabbed in the back with a knife, and the little girl had flung herself into my arms so pathetically that I scolded Charette soundly.

She had flung back, "You might as well let her grow up now. After all, wasn't her own father killed like that? She should know things that will make her less a baby! There's no need to be so overprotective of her."

"Then I suggest you do the same, Charette. Face life as it is, and perhaps you too will grow up." I was angry, and I saw her face turn pale before she turned and flounced from the room.

On the day of the funeral I sat with Aimée in her room, reading to her from a picture book. Suddenly her large round eyes looked up at me in wonderment. "Why did Michel die, mademoiselle? Why did someone want to stick a knife in him? Did they want to hurt him? Why?"

"It was an accident, my love. It is sad, Aimée, but sometimes life is like that, and we must always be prepared for it. Now I suggest that we put our books away and go out into the gardens. Let's gather some flowers for your mother. She will like that, I think."

Looking down into that beautiful face, I had to blink to keep my tears back, and I swooped her up in my arms, kissing her, then put her down. How light my heart was as I went down with her to the garden and into the courtyard.

It was when we'd gone back into the house and had placed the flowers we'd picked in the vases in my own rooms, to be taken to Danielle whenever the family arrived back from the church, that Lili brought me the sealed letter.

My hands were wet from working with the flowers and I dried them on a towel and looked at Lili. "Where did this come from, Lili?" I didn't recognize the handwriting, yet it was vaguely familiar. I was astonished.

"Madame Hortense found it in the hall, and it had your name on it. So she sent it up."

It had obviously been delivered by hand, for there was no postmark on it. But because I saw the intense look of curiosity in Lili's face, I suddenly had no wish for anyone but myself to see its contents, so I thrust it inside my pocket and waited until I was alone.

That moment came when Aimée's lunch arrived, and while she ate I took out the letter and discovered it was a very short note from Cameron Pennland!

> *My dear Tamar,*
> *Thank God you are safe! But I must be allowed to see you and to talk with you. Come alone to the old Norman fortress this afternoon, the day of the funeral. I must see you. Cameron.*
> *P.S. Please take precaution that you are alone, and be careful.*

The words danced before my eyes. It sounded dramatic and wild, and my first thought was to take it to Jean when he arrived home. We should see Cameron together, and tell him. He would understand. He deserved to be told in the right way as soon as possible. He would accept it, for I knew he was a gentleman above all things.

I reread the note. So he knew of the funeral, but how on earth had he managed to get this note into the château? How many servants in this great house led double lives? For surely one of those servants had been pressed to place it in the hall.

I was restless. From time to time I glanced at the clock. The funeral would take longer than usual, for there were masses to be said and then afterward I knew they would have to go to the Farms. I think it was then I made up my mind to meet Cameron alone. After all, I reminded myself, it was my own duty to tell him everything. I felt responsible.

I left Aimée in the care of her maid shortly after her lunch was over. She saw to it that the little girl would rest. It did not take me long to change into my riding habit, and when I went down the stairs and cut into the stableyard, I found there were very few servants about, and the stables were almost deserted. I saddled the horse I'd been used to, a fine chestnut mare we called Lothair, and took the path I was now familiar with away from the château, skirting the village and hurrying on toward the cliffs.

The ride was long and my heart thudded uncomfortably when I came in sight of the old Norman castle. How had I thought I could come here alone and descend that rope ladder to the ledge? I must have been insane to believe I could do such a thing!

It was Lothair who decided for me, for he went

on ahead on the path, and when we arrived at the top of the cliff, I felt a compelling desire to run away as fast as I could.

As I started to turn around, a figure stepped out of the trees, and my heart seemed to stop in fright. It was the leather-clad figure of Nicolas, a smile of surprise on his handsome face.

"So you have come, mademoiselle." He laughed as he took and held the reins of my mount. His words took me by surprise, and I was indignant for some reason, unexplained even to myself. Some inner instinct warned me not to trust this man. I dimly recalled Jean's warning after we'd visited the caves that day. They came back like a shot in the dark. ". . . Be careful around Nicolas. Don't trust him. He is like a viper!"

I sat on my mount, aloof, and stared down at him in distrust, and for the instant our eyes met, he seemed hesitant.

"Will you not dismount, mademoiselle? I will tether your horse for you in the trees, *s'il vous plaît*."

"What do you know of my coming here?" I asked, angry that I'd let him see my fear and distrust.

White teeth flashed, and the long dark eyes were bold upon my face. "You are distrustful of me, mademoiselle," he laughed. "But did you not receive a note to come here?" He was playing a game, I thought. So he knew about it. Perhaps it was he who would take me to Cameron.

Still, I hesitated. The instinct to flee was strong, but even in this I could see he was laughing at my fear, and I made an effort to calm myself so that he could not take advantage of me.

"Very well. Take me to him." I believed I saw a gleam of victory in his expression, and as he helped me dismount, I wondered if I were mad to put myself into his cunning hands. I clutched my riding crop instinctively, and stepped back from him.

He merely laughed and moved off into the trees with my horse. When he came back, he did not go off into the brush to get the ladder as Jean had done but gestured for me to follow him to the cliff's edge. I did so with a trembling heart. He went first over the edge, that laughter in his eyes, as if he knew my every thought. I was determined I should not allow him to see my fear any longer, and so I followed him over the cliff and down the ladder that was already there.

A sudden gust of wind bringing unexpected rain hit us as we stepped down on that ledge, and a single gull soared upward, crying out stridently.

"This rain will make the ledge slippery, mademoiselle. We must hurry, but please follow me carefully and closely," Nicolas said, and then turned to go before me.

The rain swept in blindly, and although we had a shelter overhead, it couldn't protect us from the driving wind. Then Nicolas parted the curtain of swaying vines and entered into the musty entrance to the caves. I was drenched, and when he followed in after me, he hurriedly lit some of the candles and handed me one. Without another word he turned and began walking through the chain of caves and tunnels, and it was all I could do to keep him in sight as I ran after him.

We had not yet reached the tunnel that would take me under the moat when I caught up with him in the last cave. He was waiting, and I noticed he'd placed his candle on a ledge, and was busy at a table. Even here, I noticed, it was habitable, with a thick straw mattress in one corner, a charcoal brazier which was glowing with embers of a fire, and several blackened pots there, one of which he moved over the fire.

I assumed then that this was where I'd be meeting Cameron. It occurred to me that Neville too might appear, and some of my immediate fears left me.

For a moment I stood in the cave's entrance, taking it all in, and with his back to me Nicolas said, "Make yourself comfortable while we wait, eh, mademoiselle?" He laughed. "We'll have some coffee in a few minutes. Use that crate to sit on, if you like."

I preferred to stand, but I eased into the room, less apprehensive now, and tried to brush the dampness from my skirt. I took off my hat and shook it, then replaced it on my head, thankful for the scarf I'd worn with it. I fervently hoped that Cameron wouldn't take long in getting here, and I now had deep anxieties about riding back to the château in that blinding rain along the steep cliff paths I'd come over. It had been a folly, my coming here, and I was regretting it more and more as the seconds passed.

Nicolas turned around and I knew by his bold look that no woman would ever be completely safe in his company alone. He lifted his eyebrows, an all-knowing look in those eyes, and with a trace of mockery in his voice, he said, "So there is to be a hasty wedding, eh, Mademoiselle Tamar? A funeral, and now a wedding." He laughed, and it seemed to echo around us.

I shuddered involuntarily. "It must be very difficult for your family to bear this untimely death of your uncle," I said, trying to ignore the remark about the wedding. "Have you no idea who might have wanted to murder Michel?"

He shrugged. "Plenty of people had their reasons, I suspect. Michel was not popular."

"Your family is quite close, are they not?" I wanted him to talk, and not about Jean and me. "I mean, you were together in the Resistance? Your father and mother, as well as Michel? Were you with them too, Nicolas?"

He sat down on a packing box, and even from where I stood, he smelled of leather and tobacco. He took out a pouch and began to stuff a pipe with its aromatic contents. But if I thought he was going to give me a detailed account of the history of his family, I was quite mistaken.

"They are considered quite a closely knit family. They will bury Michel today, and then they will accept what is. That is the Cottereau family. They have mixed well with the nobility of the Rouvroy family, in business and in politics, but not in marriage. No one ever thought of marriage between the two families. That was Michel's big mistake, wanting to marry the Marquis de Rouvroy's beautiful daughter, to be part of that family of aristocrats. And do you know?" He laughed that wicked laugh of his, raising an eyebrow at me. "He never really had her, not once in those six months. He was cheated even in his marriage to her, always consumed by that jealousy of the man who gave her a daughter." His laugh mocked the uncle who now lay dead in the cemetery.

I despised him for it, and I wanted to strike him, to wipe that smirk off his face for speaking so ill of my niece. How contemptuous he was, how arrogant. I reasoned then that he could not know of Danielle's real marriage to Neville.

"But you, Mademoiselle Tamar. You have won favor in the eyes of the young Marquis de Rouvroy, *n'est-ce pas?*" he said softly as he came over and stood beside me. "*Ma petite* Charette has given her favors to me, but not in the marriage bed! Never that. Perhaps mademoiselle will give me a taste of her favors, eh?"

I had taken a step backward, but found myself up against a stone wall, trapped. I met his eyes defiantly, but in the next instant he reached out and pulled me to him, and I had no time even to think of fighting this brutal animal, yet I gave him a push with all my strength. When he was off balance, I struck out with my riding crop, hitting him full across the eyes, blinding him, and then I ran madly to the nearest entrance. It was only when I saw a pale light ahead of me that I realized I was moving through the narrow tunnel under the moat. But I could not go back; Nicolas was there and he would . . .

I didn't think what he would do, but even now it passed through my mind that he would have me at his mercy in this place, for I had no protection whatsoever. Jean would never guess that I had come here, and I would be hunted down by Nicolas without a prayer of being rescued.

The appalling thought that night would come and I would still be in this place numbed me. Where was Cameron? Surely he was here! Hadn't the note been from him? Why had he not met me instead of Nicolas? I was thinking this as I ran up the few steps into that antechamber beneath the fortress.

It was only when I stopped to think for a second that I knew the answer. Of course! Cameron had asked me to meet him in the old castle fortress, not the caves! I made for those stairs as fast as I could.

I climbed to the top, to a narrow landing where a deep Norman arch formed a doorway with a heavy oak door that gave way when I pushed it.

I found myself in a large courtyard open to the rain. I stopped, wondering where Cameron would be.

The hands that grabbed me from behind were like steel, and a scream rose in my throat, terror piercing my heart as I was spun about.

"Tamar! Thank God you're here at last!" It was Cameron Pennland.

Relief poured through me, draining me of my strength. "Cameron! How you frightened me!" I tried to laugh, but my voice was trembling, and I might have fallen had his hands not been holding me.

"I believed you might not have received the note. You took so long." The blue eyes were all over my face, accusingly, flashing in the strange yellowish twilight darkened with rain. "My God, but what you must have been put through at the hands of that devil, the Frenchman! I tell you now, I'll kill the man who dared touch you!" He pulled me to him and the strength of his body made my trembling stop at once.

"Oh, Cameron!" I tried to stand back from him, but he held on to me firmly. "You don't understand—not really. It was not like that . . . at all." I could see that he believed I might have come to some humiliating torture. "That's why I came here, to tell you about Jean de Rouvroy. . . ."

"Jean de Rouvroy is the man I intend to settle the score with, my dear! I shall not rest until I've had it out with that . . . scoundrel! You can't know what I went through after that night—"

I pulled myself out of his hands, taking a deep swallow, my throat tight and dry. I would have to tell him, and it would hurt him, I realized. I saw in his eyes a possessiveness of me—that same possessiveness I remembered on the night of the ball when we were dancing.

I faced him, but he moved toward me and said, "Let's get out of this rain, shall we? I have a small place ready for you. I won't let you go back to the château, Tamar. I'm never going to let you out of my sight again, once this is over."

Before I could protest, he took my arm and hurried me across that old stone-paved courtyard into a cloister. At once I felt the warmth, and glanced about me; I could see every effort had been made to make this room habitable, with a table and two chairs, a narrow bed with folded blankets, and a small charcoal stove. Despite the damp chill of the afternoon, the room was relatively warm.

I had to admit this came as a surprise. "Does Neville stay here with you, Cameron? I thought—" I didn't finish, for he was busy at the stove making coffee. I waited; I thought Neville would be staying in the grotto with Nicolas. Then why was Cameron here? I was bewildered, full of so many unanswered questions.

I stood still, watching him as he poured coffee into two thick earthen mugs, then replaced the pan on the stove. He looked up at me and gestured with his hand for me to come and take one of the chairs.

Suddenly I realized I didn't know this man at all. He was a complete stranger to me, and I felt a strain between us, a barrier that I could not penetrate.

I sat down in the chair he held for me, and then he sat across from me. "I want to explain—" I began.

"You don't have to, Tamar. I know what you must have gone through since that night. But now it's over. I have you here with me where I can look after you. Look. I am going to Paris in a very few days' time, and I shall take you there. Then we can be married, and I will take you back to Penn Hall where you should be right now! By God," he exploded with a dark scowl. "How I'd like to get my hands around the neck of that Frenchman!"

"Cameron," I said slowly, determined now that he must know what I came to tell him. "How did you get the note to me at the château?" Our eyes met across the yellow gleam of the room.

"It was easy. Servants are always useful, especially if one knows them as I do."

I was astonished and he laughed softly. "You needn't worry. I took all the precautions."

"Have you been here before?"

"Of course. I thought you knew."

"Knew what?" Why did my heart hammer so loudly, I thought.

It was his turn to look surprised. "I thought you knew that I was here with Neville before, helping with the Resistance at Quiberon."

Something lodged like a pebble in the outskirts of my mind, yet it escaped me just then.

"Nicolas Cottereau—" Again I stopped, hesitating. "He knew about the note you sent today?"

He looked surprised again. "Why, no. No. I'm sure he couldn't have known about it. Why do you ask?"

"He was waiting for me on the cliff outside. . . ." I did not wish to relate just what I'd run from.

"The devil you say!" He seemed as puzzled as I was. "Well, perhaps he knows the servant well enough . . ."

"The note was sealed. How could he have known?"

For a while, he was deep in thought.

"I must tell you this now, Cameron. I came alone, because I must tell you I cannot stay here with you. I must get back to the château tonight. You see," I said, moving my tongue over my dry lips, taking a sip of the thick black coffee, "I am engaged to marry Jean de Rouvroy. It all happened so quickly, so unexpectedly. But we are going to be married in a few days, within the week, in fact. You must understand. I don't wish to . . . hurt you, but I cannot marry you, Cameron. Not now, not after . . . Jean."

At first I believe he hadn't heard what I'd been saying, for he only stared at me. Then he reached over and covered my hand with one of his own. "My dear Tamar. I will not allow you even to think you have to marry that man! My God! To think how he used you as bait to bring Neville back to Brittany! The man is a devil, I tell you, and then to hear you say that he is forcing you to marry him! By God, but he has nerve!"

I pulled my hand free. "It's not like that at all, Cameron," I said strongly. "I am not being forced into marriage. I accepted of my own free will."

He frowned. "What you're telling me is that he seduced you. Is that it?"

"Listen to me, Cameron. It is not that way at all, you must believe me. I love Jean de Rouvroy! I want to be his wife, do you hear me? He did not seduce me, not in that sense!"

He stared at me, unbelieving, as if he'd just been betrayed. "Then what of our plans? You were promised to me, remember?" I heard the hurt beneath his pride, and I was smitten with guilt.

"That time belongs to another world in which I no longer exist, Cameron," I said softly, trying to find the words that would be kind, but truth that he would accept.

"Nonsense. I know you, Tamar. You are trying to be dramatic, like Marietta. What can that

Frenchman be to you other than your abductor? You can't know what love is, not with a man like that!"

"You are mistaken, Cameron," I said calmly. "I love Jean. Nothing can change that." I knew my eyes were blazing, and my color heightened. I wasn't going to allow anyone, no matter who it was, to tarnish my love for Jean or his for me."

"Well, by God, we shall see about that!" He stood up. "I will change it, and now. You belong to me, Tamar Columb, and I won't ever let you forget that!"

So here it was, that possessiveness I'd seen in him that night of the ball. But I was not afraid, not now, not for myself. He stood over me, his eyes stormy with all the inner passions of jealousy and hate for the one man who had changed the course of my life and his.

"We will slip out of here and go to Paris at dawn. I have arranged for passage on the carriage from Brest. I even have your papers ready. You will be my wife, and when we do get to Paris, I've arranged a wedding at our consulate for us, a civil ceremony, but one that will stand firm. I want to get you safely out of Brittany first. Paris will be gay enough, bright enough for a honeymoon, I think, Tamar." His anger cooled, and in its place I saw calm determination.

"I'm not going with you, Cameron." I looked up at him steadily. If my heart was missing several beats and thudding where it should not, I was determined that he should not be allowed to know that.

8

"My dear Tamar," he said, his voice full of authority and self-confidence, "you have no choice now in this matter. I am going to look after you just as Neville has entreated me to do. We are going to be married, and in the end we shall go back to Cornwall." He placed his hand on my shoulder rather heavily, and I shrank from his touch. It was as if I suddenly found this man repulsive, and I could not control my reaction.

He saw it, and he removed his hand, staring at me strangely. That had touched the core of him; I was aware of it just as he was.

I stood up and walked away from him, holding my coffee mug. "You said you were here in Brittany with Neville during the Resistance, Cameron. Were you an . . . agent then, as Neville was?"

He nodded, in a mechanical way. "Yes. Of course."

"Did you have a code name? Like Neville's

Marc Renoire?" I sipped the coffee, watching him, and he frowned.

"Yes. I went under the name André Duhamel. And those are the papers, forged of course, that we shall use getting through the Republican lines, such as they are. Monsieur André Duhamel, a wine merchant from Bordeaux, and his wife, going to Paris to have a bit of holiday. It wasn't easy to get the pass for you, but a little persuasion has made it possible."

"Tell me about that time—Quiberon Bay. Was that not the night the cause was lost to General Hoche?" That tiny recollection that had escaped my mind before now came to me in a landslide as I recalled Danielle's words. "Uncle Henri came to Brittany, and brought with him another English agent whose name I only knew as André . . ." And Cameron was that English agent. I should have guessed it before now.

"Yes. It all happened that way, unfortunately. But that is all over now, and I don't want to be a part of this new cause for a Bourbon who was making empty promises. I want only to get you back to England with me, Tamar."

"Did you know Danielle de Rouvroy? The niece of Henri de Rouvroy?" I asked, and I watched as he drank his coffee.

"Yes, I knew her. She was quite beautiful. I believe she and Neville had at one time been friendly. Or so it seemed to me. But she sure did fool me, as well as her uncle, that night of all nights!"

"What do you mean? What night? At Quiberon?"

He shrugged, shifting himself and sitting down on the edge of the table. "The night everything was planned to go ahead with the infamous, ill-fated landing of all those poor devils. There was a traitor among us, and as far as I know he has not ever been discovered. Treachery was everywhere that night, so it was no surprise when Hoche scoured the whole region for the remaining *Chouans*."

"Weren't you one of them?"

He laughed, scornfully I thought. "Not I. No. Neville was one of their main leaders, from the English side. I came down from Paris, directly from London, and just happened to be on the tail end of that tragedy. I wonder that Neville never spoke of it to you. Marietta never knew either." He smiled. "She's set her cap for your brother, and if he gets out of this alive, I dare say she will have her way."

She will be disappointed when she discovers differently, I told myself, turning away. "What happened to Danielle de Rouvroy that night? You mentioned that she fooled you and her uncle as well? How do you mean?"

"For one thing, had she been *my* woman, I should never have allowed her to go with those . . . *tarts* to tease those officers. My God, but she was a beautiful woman! Everything about her spoke of her well-trained background, aristocratic to the last word! Everything a gentleman would want. I will say this, Tamar. I wanted her, and I wanted to marry her, so I thought. But she would have nothing to do with me. It puzzled me, for when she offered to go to the officers' camp that night, she clearly showed just what kind of woman she really was. Even if she was of noble birth, she had that . . . French 'looseness' about her that made her as common as the other women she went along with."

"What happened?" I felt the breath go out of me, as if I were hearing a completely different story of a different time and place.

He shrugged. "She went to them, and she deserved what she bargained for. I believe she died in the end. Men will be men anywhere, and Hoche's officers were no better than animals. The women were betrayed; they were used then, in the vilest of ways. But that is war, and those women deserved what they got."

He had no sympathy. "Were you with Henri de Rouvroy? Or with Neville?"

"I was with Henri most of that night, and then, when it all failed, I met with Neville, and we made our escape. We had to. We didn't even know what had become of Henri, not then, not right away. It was all so hopeless, and we were fortunate to escape with our lives."

We were so engrossed in our conversation that we failed to hear the door open at the other end of the room. It was only when a strong voice spoke that we turned, startled. It was the tall lean figure of Henri de Rouvroy, roughly clad in leather with a heavy dark cloak around his shoulders and a wide-brimmed hat over his head. He was a far cry from the dignified Marquis de Rouvroy I had seen earlier in the morning as he rode away in the carriage with Danielle and Jean.

"André Duhamel! *Mon Dieu!* What in God's name are you doing in this old fortress?"

Cameron strode across the room. "It's been a long time, *mon ami!*" He laughed boldly, clasping the outstretched hand, and both men slapped each other on the shoulders in camaraderie.

"But this is a surprise," Henri said. "André. So it was you who came with Marc? I never thought to see you again after Quiberon." He glanced beyond Cameron's shoulders to where I stood, the dark eyes a study of puzzlement as they rested briefly on my face.

"*Mais oui,* who else?" Cameron said, pleasure lighting up in his expression. "That rascal of a nephew of yours had Marc and me in quite a state, abducting my fiancée like that, just to get Marc back here!"

"Your fiancée?" The marquis looked to me for an answer. I moved across the room, keeping clear of Cameron's reach, and said, "Monsieur le Marquis, Cameron Pennland and I were having a betrothal ball at Columb Manor when Jean came that night. But since that time I have given my heart and my word to Jean. I must make Cameron understand that. You must help me to convince him that Jean and I are to be married in a few days. I came here at Cameron's request, hoping he would understand that Jean's intentions toward me are honorable ones."

I heard the sharp intake of Cameron's breath as I finished speaking, and in that silence I heard the pounding of my heart as it matched that of the rain pelting down on the courtyard outside. I did not allow my glance to waver from the eyes of the marquis. That I had chosen to place my cause in his hands surprised even me, but I couldn't allow him to believe that Cameron was anything more to me than a neighbor now, an old friend, no matter what else happened.

"*Ma chère* Tamar," the marquis said, taking both my hands in his own gloved ones. "Of course Monsieur Pennland will fully understand when I tell him of the feelings Jean has for you. It is for this very reason *I* have come here and not Jean. We must have peace among us if we are to work together. *Mais oui.*" He smiled down into my eyes. "We must hurry back to the château. We can't make you late for your own wedding, and it is to be early in the morning, you see. So Pierre François has arranged it." His hands were strong and warm as they pressed mine.

"But, how?" I exclaimed, marveling at what I'd just heard him say. "How was it arranged so soon? And how could you know I was here?" He'd seen the joy leap in my eyes, I guessed, when he spoke of the wedding, and now he seemed to be laughing.

"Charette tells all, hoping to snare Jean once and for all with her little intrigues. It seems she had you followed, Tamar. But you needn't worry about her any more. I've decided she should go to stay with an old friend of her mother's in Paris. Perhaps she needs a woman's touch." He sighed a bit unhappily, then was silent.

"So this is the way it is, Tamar?" Cameron said at last.

I nodded. "Yes. I'm sorry, Cameron. But I love Jean."

"Very well then. The best man wins. There is to be a wedding, then?" His eyes went to the marquis.

The marquis said, "Yes. In the church very early in the morning. The happy couple is to go to Paris. It is all arranged. And if you are ready, Tamar, we shall get on our way. André." He stopped and waited, shifting his cloak back over one shoulder.

It came as a shock to see the gun that hung from the marquis's belt under that cloak, and I realized he had meant to kill the man if necessary, before he knew the situation and that the man was André Duhamel.

The two men stared at each other. "Marc will be there at the church, in a disguise, of course. If you want to come, we can arrange it so. But we must be careful. The chief of police has a cordon around the château and Farms."

"The unfortunate murder of Michel Cottereau must have been a drawback to your cause, I suppose?" Cameron said seriously.

"Hmm, it was a . . . shock to us. You know that he was my niece's husband?" The brown eyes were direct and watchful.

"Your niece? You mean Danielle de Rouvroy?" It was his turn to show complete surprise. "I somehow believed she didn't survive that ordeal at the officers' camp."

Henri de Rouvroy grimaced. "She barely got away. But, yes, Danielle survived it, only to marry Michel Cottereau six months ago, and now he is in his grave."

Cameron was silent and thoughtful to this, and

the marquis took my arm and led me toward the door. "We must be leaving, if we're to make it by nightfall. You know how to get in touch, should you want to come, André. Be careful."

Cameron only nodded. He watched us, his eyes narrowed, and I thought he would say some word, or even wish me well, but he did not, lifting his hand in a gesture toward the marquis. As we went out, I could not rid myself of some deep guilt that I had brought Cameron pain.

When we arrived at the grotto, Jean came out with Neville behind him, practically running. I broke away and ran toward him, and Jean caught me in his arms and held me close. My face was wet with tears of joy, and he was kissing them away. It was only a moment, but it seemed like eternity and I would have gladly allowed it to be so, standing within the sweet protection of his embrace, with his heart beating as rapidly as mine.

But it was Neville who broke the spell. "We must hurry. Tamar? Are you all right?" he asked needlessly, and grinned. "I can see that for myself, of course. But, you . . . saw Cameron?"

I knew by the glances between Jean and my brother that Jean had been properly informed of Cameron's existence. So I only nodded, reminding myself of my gratitude toward my brother for speaking to Jean, and that Jean had understood.

Behind us, Nicolas appeared from the grotto, and the marquis went to him and began conversing in low but rapid French. When Nicolas turned to face Jean and me, I cringed when I saw the huge welt across his face that my riding crop had made.

But whatever the man felt toward me in that moment, he disguised it with bold mockery, more ruthless than ever. I did nothing to encourage any form of greeting between us, and decided I would not mention what had happened to Jean, or to anyone else. I would let the whole encounter drop.

So it was that we took our leave of the fortress, with Nicolas standing behind, his arms crossed over the broad chest, watching us depart as if the whole interlude had provided some amusement.

It was late when Jean and I slipped through the gates into the courtyard, leaving Neville with the marquis to go through the secret passage and through the dungeons where Neville would remain hidden. It had been arranged to look as if Jean and I had met out on the cliffs and were now returning, after having been caught by the storm and thus kept out later than usual.

The house was exceptionally quiet, and Jean went with me immediately to my rooms, closing the door behind us. He turned to me, holding my arm.

"I can't tell you my fears when I knew you'd gone out there alone, Tamar. You must never do that again."

I smiled at his concern. "I promise I shall act more wisely in the future. It was just that it seemed the right thing to do. I know now it wasn't. I should have waited for you."

"Yes." He kissed my cheek, and then my lips. Then we clung to each other in a sudden rush of longing. He touched my face, tracing my cheek with his finger. "I love you, Tamar. Don't ever forget that," he said, looking deeply into my eyes.

"Never, never." His kisses told me that, and gave me courage. "I wanted to have you with me when I told Cameron about us, Jean. To tell him together—" I stopped, for with a sudden shudder of fear, I remembered the murderous look in Cameron's eyes, and I was glad now that I'd been alone, and Jean safe from his wrath.

"I hadn't an idea that he meant so much to you."

"He didn't—ever!"

"You were going to marry him."

"It was an . . . agreement. Not love."

"You didn't tell me about him," he teased, looking into my eyes.

"I didn't need to. He was never important. I even forgot about him, because I didn't love him."

"You are not sorry, then, that I abducted you in the most abominable manner, from the very scene of the ball?"

"And carried me off to your château to hold me prisoner?" I laughed. "How indignant I was, yet I shouldn't have wanted to be returned to that scene you dragged me from."

"I wanted you to be my prisoner, from that first moment I saw you."

"In the study, you mean?"

"No. On the afternoon of the day I had my men scout around Columb Manor. You were walking on the cliff path, staring at the sea, with such an expression of deep thought that I wondered then why so enchanting a young woman would look that way. What were you thinking, my dear Tamar?"

Surprised, I could only look at him for an instant in silence when I remembered that sunny afternoon which now seemed a lifetime ago. "Do you know, it was . . . *you* I was thinking of, Jean."

"Me?" His expression was incredulous.

"I had found the locket, you see. The locket which had your likeness inside, along with Danielle's. I even had it in my pocket, and every now and then, I would take it out and look at it, wondering who you were and where you were, and what had become of you."

He was staring at me, uncomprehending. "The locket? But that's impossible. Utterly impossible! How did you come to have it?"

"I discovered it in a garden at Columb Manor, Jean. When Neville saw it, he denied ever having seen it and believed it might have belonged to my mother," I said, explaining what had happened as Jean walked over to the window, staring blindly into the night.

"Where is the locket now?" he asked quietly.

"Danielle has it."

"You returned it to her?"

"Yes. Of course. And Jean," I said, coming up behind him, "I think you should know the truth—"

"The truth? I already know the truth, don't I?" He looked angry.

"I don't think you do." I took a deep breath and plunged in, telling him everything I knew about Danielle and Neville. "So you see, they are married, my brother and your sister. And

Aimée—Aimée has a father. Neville Columb is her true father."

For a long moment he said nothing, but kept staring into the rain outside the window. "How can you or Danielle or Neville explain the locket there at Columb Manor?"

"We can't. That is the mystery. I found it, but who could have placed it there?" We looked at each other for a long time, hearing the crackling of the flames in the fireplace.

He came to me and touched my cheek. "We shall leave it at that, *ma chère*. I'm certain there is an explanation, but we'll not worry over it now. The important thing is for us to get out of these wet clothes and have a hot dinner. Pierre François will be wanting to speak with us both, too. You don't mind the hasty wedding, do you?"

"Of course not. I find it rather exciting. Where is Pierre François? Is he to be here at the château?"

"He is here now, yes." We were both silent for a moment, reflecting on this event that would change our futures.

Jean left me then, and I rang for Lili to bring hot water, stripping off my riding habit, thankful indeed that I'd had the cover of a thick wool cloak the marquis had thought to bring along with him to the old fortress.

I soaked away the stains of my adventure, and hardly had I stepped from the bath with my robe wrapped around me, when Danielle came into my rooms. She hurried to me, kissing my cheek, her eyes all glowing and dark.

"Jean told me you were back, Tamar. I can't

tell you of my anguish for your safety, and it's a good thing that Jean and Uncle Henri were able to shake the truth out of Charette! But thank God! She may see some sense now."

"Where is she? Charette?"

"She is in her room, and Maurice has been with her most of the time. Maurice has been wonderful, under the circumstances. No doubt he will have his hands full with her when they go off to Paris tomorrow. You know, I think she will like it there, being in fashionable Paris with a certain amount of freedom. Yes, it is best that she go to Madame Louise Passy, her mother's friend."

"Then I'm glad for her and for everyone," I said and meant it, hoping that this would be the solution to Charette's problems.

"Your wedding is to take place so very early, Tamar. Now, I wonder if you would allow me to make a suggestion as far as your wedding gown is concerned?"

"Of course," I answered. My wedding gown. I had not given it a thought. "I could wear my ball gown—"

She held up her hand, quieting me. "I want you to wear my mother's bridal gown, Tamar. I believe Jean would be pleased too. She had it placed aside for me, and although I hadn't a chance to wear it on that first occasion, I plan to wear it myself tonight, during a very special ceremony." She blushed and I grasped her hands.

"Danielle! What are you saying?" I laughed happily.

She nodded. "I've asked Pierre François if he would allow my husband and me to renew our marriage vows this very night in a very secret ceremony, Tamar dear. He already knows our situation, of course, but he thinks this would right everything in the eyes of the church for our little Aimée. I want to wear my mother's bridal gown for this, and you shall have it afterward, if you will do us the honor of accepting it."

Our eyes touched in an immediate understanding, and I pulled her into my arms and we embraced, tears rushing to our eyes. For a while we just clung to each other, not speaking, for words were not needed.

After a moment we both stood back, wiping our eyes, and Danielle said, "Now. Please go ahead with your toilette. We shall be quite formal tonight, for we are having a small celebration, outwardly for you and Jean, but privately for . . . Neville and me." She said my brother's name with an accent that was quite charming, I thought, and she smiled, her full mouth curving ever so gently. "Afterward, we can try on the gown, but I think it will be easily adjusted to suit us. Sister Magdaleine will be here from the convent. She is one of the Cottereau sisters, you know. Michel's youngest sister."

"No. I didn't know," I said, astonished. For I remembered Nicolas had been conferring with one of the nuns that day at the convent which seemed so long ago.

She nodded her head. "Yes. Sister Magdaleine has been more than a friend to me. She cared for me during that terrible time when I believed I'd lost Marc. She was with me when Aimée was born, so she will come tonight. We will go into the secret chamber where Neville is hiding now, and we'll take our wedding cup and say our vows. I want to be Neville Columb's wife. Marc Renoire is . . . of the past."

"Then I am glad," I said. "It's all so romantic, Danielle. Neville truly deserves someone like you in his life now. He has missed much, I believe, by being without you. I'm very, very happy for you both. And I am glad we are sisters."

"Thank you, Tamar. How truly blessed we both are!"

She glanced around us, then said, "Hurry and dress now." She left me. Lili had laid out my green velvet gown and when I'd arranged my hair I glanced into the mirror. A woman in love stared back at me, and I made myself believe that nothing could go wrong from this moment on.

When Jean met me at the foot of the staircase, he came up and kissed me gently, pressing a velvet case into my hands. "This is for you. An engagement gift I've wanted to give you even before now."

I opened the box and saw an emerald necklace. Never in my life had I seen anything so lovely. Maurice was watching with intense pleasure on his face, and Charette looked on enviously, but Jean ignored her and took the jewels from their case and fastened them around my neck. When his lips touched my neck, I wished I could kiss him lingeringly, even in front of his family.

"The last of the de Rouvroy jewels, Tamar. But what justice you do to them!" exclaimed Maurice. "May I kiss the bride-to-be, Jean? I will anyway, then ask later, and then face the duel!" He laughed and moved to take me into his arms and kissed my lips. It was all in fun, but for Charette it was not.

The poppy red of her silk gown offset the beauty of her dark eyes and hair, but she pouted and said under her breath, "I can't think why Jean would give them to her, when they belong to the family!"

Maurice looked at his sister, frowning. "But she is part of the family now, *ma petite* Charette. Tamar is Jean's choice and she will be his bride in just a few hours."

For a moment they looked at each other, and somehow it tore my heart apart to watch them. I knew Jean was watching too.

"She isn't a bride yet," Charette said in a small voice.

"What the devil do you mean by that?" Maurice said, and I could sense the girl's sudden shrinking as his hand shot out and grabbed her wrist.

At once she became obedient and embarrassed. "I'm sorry. Yes. I'm sorry." She looked up at me, but I could not tell if she meant what she was saying. "I am to say I'm sorry to you, Tamar. If you can forgive me, please do. But I do not want you to be Jean's bride. Not ever." I thought she might have run off had not her brother held her.

It was such an unexpected outburst that it stunned us all. For a moment no one could say anything, and then I moved toward her, holding out my hand, but she ignored it completely.

"Then I accept your apology, Charette. I hope we shall become friends one day, and then perhaps you will accept me as Jean's wife." In my happiness, I wanted everyone, Charette included, to share my joy.

But something in her eyes and in the way she held her head seemed to deny even this offer of friendship. It was a strained moment, and she looked away from me to the stairway where Danielle and the marquis stood on the landing.

So we stepped aside, Jean and I, as Danielle floated down the stairs now on the arm of the marquis. How correct and distinguished he was, I thought, as if he had everything under complete control. There seemed to be a new closeness between Danielle and her uncle, and when she came down, I noticed the locket she wore about her neck.

"Oh, Danielle," Charette cried. "What a beautiful necklace! Since Jean has parted with the last of the de Rouvroy gems, I did not know you had other such jewels. I've not seen it before, have I?"

Danielle laughed, her eyes glowing with her joy that could no longer be kept secret. "It is an heirloom, Charette, and one that has been lost to me for several years, in fact. But it belonged to my mother and grandmother before her. My mother always wore it, and she gave it to me before . . ." And here she stopped, looking at Jean and the marquis. "Before she died," she finished softly.

Maurice laughed. "Then you are fortunate, cousin," he said. "I marvel that all the de Rouvroy jewels are gone but now that Jean has given Tamar the emeralds, there's nothing to be given to Charette or the woman I might wed some day." He was teasing, but there was a trace of malice in his voice, I believed, and I looked at the marquis to see how this affected him.

He did not seem disturbed by it at all. "All those jewels were taken in exile with the family, Maurice. But I dare say something might turn up for you when the time comes. Neither of you will be getting married in the near future, though, so let's not worry about it now, all right?" He looked around at all of us. "Let us go together into the *grande salle,* for I believe Jacques is waiting with our drinks. We have a few celebrations to give toast to. Take my arm, *ma petite* Charette." He held his arm out and she seemed glad to take it. The four of us followed them into the *grande salle,* where we settled comfortably around a blazing fire.

From time to time during the evening, I caught the marquis's eyes upon me, and then on Jean. I sensed that he too was marking time, and whenever I found the glances pass between him and Danielle, I was certain of it.

I was certain also that neither Maurice nor Charette knew about Neville and Danielle. I knew that everything—all the careful plans and hopes for the restoration of the Bourbon king to the throne—depended upon keeping those plans secret. To allow Maurice de Rouvroy to know of key positions and of English agents who were helping the freedom fighters to get another foothold in Brittany was completely out of the question, even if he was a member of the family.

Even so, I wondered just how much he did know, and how much he would reveal if the opportunity came.

It was just after midnight when, after we'd had black coffee and brandy, the marquis asked us to rise and follow him. Jacques promptly locked all the connecting doors to the small dining room, and the marquis lifted the thick tapestry that covered one wall, and to my surprise pressed a button in the intricately paneled wall. Part of that wall slid silently aside, revealing a door. The marquis took a key from his waistcoat pocket and fitted it in the lock, and it swung open. He stood aside and motioned for all of us to go through. Oddly enough, as I stared at the faces of everyone there, it was only Maurice, Charette, and I who seemed surprised.

The curé went before us, followed by Sister Magdaleine, then Danielle and I and Charette, with the marquis coming last after Jean, Maurice, and even Jacques. We entered a dimly lit passage and then went through another door into a small chapel anteroom. Candles in old iron sconces burned softly, and pools of light touched our faces as we walked into the small stone room.

The curé walked ahead of us and asked us all to sit in the chairs around a table, and he moved out of sight, with only a nod toward the marquis.

It was Maurice who spoke, and his voice sounded eerie and hollow. "I didn't even suspect this place existed, Uncle Honoré," he laughed. "This place would have been perfect for the fugitives during the Resistance. I suspect now that my own father used it to smuggle in arms and ammunition that was reportedly stashed away somewhere." But I could see he was a little disturbed now as to why we were here. "Did you know about this place, Jean?" he asked.

Jean only nodded in the affirmative, because the marquis silenced him with a look. And he himself began to speak. "Maurice, I wanted you to witness this because I must tell you and Charette . . . everything." The two young people looked at him blankly, as if he were getting ready to tell them of their doom.

As no one spoke, the marquis went on, "When you both go from here, Maurice, you will be going with information that could send us all to the guillotine, but you must know the full truth."

Maurice blanched suddenly; even in the tawny light I could see how pale he went. I was almost positive that what the marquis was going to reveal was not what Maurice expected, and Charette's expression told me the same.

Dark eyes met dark eyes. "Uncle Honoré—" he began, embarrassed, but the marquis silenced him with a gesture of his uplifted hand.

"*S'il vous plaît,* my boy, Maurice. I want you and the others to hear this. Pierre François is here to bear out this truth for the records, as well as Sister Magdaleine with her undying loyalty toward the family de Rouvroy and to Danielle. We have agreed that it is time now for the whole truth to be known. For I believe Charette and you, Maurice, have been cheated more than anyone else in this family."

Danielle stood up and went over to her uncle and kissed his cheek. "Thank you," she said softly before sitting down beside Charette.

"Tonight Danielle is to be reunited with the

man she loves and believed dead all these years since that fateful night at Quiberon. Her husband, the English agent known as Marc Renoire, but whose name is Neville Columb, the father of our little Aimée, is waiting for her in the recesses of this old chapel. They are to say their vows again with the blessings of the Church, and we are going to witness it. Maurice, Charette—" he looked at his two children, and I could tell just how moved he was in this moment of truth and I felt Jean's hand press mine tightly, "I am not your Uncle Honoré, the Marquis de Rouvroy, but an impostor. I am Henri, his brother, and your own father."

For a second it seemed as if time had stopped, and suddenly Charette ran to the arms of her father, crying, "Papa! Oh, Papa! *Mon père*—" she sobbed, and the strong arms went around her protectively. I saw his own eyes were moist as they shut tight and he buried his face in her hair.

Maurice rose and went to him too, and it was such a tender scene of reunion that I turned to Jean and found his eyes were as moist as mine. We all stood up and went to embrace and to congratulate them, and Sister Magdaleine wept along with us.

It was Maurice who asked, "But how? Why?" There was a mixture of both pleasure and astonishment on his face and in his voice.

Henri de Rouvroy sat down slowly, and with great patience explained the complicated events that led to their present situation. I admired his handling of the touchy subjects involved, especially when his children asked why they'd not been told long ago. Charette and Maurice were both quite young at the time their father switched his identity, and they could not have been expected to keep such an important secret.

"I had to make an immediate decision," he said. "You both were abroad, and I felt I could look after you both here at the château. You must forgive me for this, Maurice. Jean learned the truth right away, and I couldn't deceive Danielle. She had already been told by Sister Magdaleine of the massacre at the church. It was a time we can never forget."

In the silence that followed, I noticed Charette still clung to her father's arm, a new light shining in her eyes. How she had needed a father, I thought at once, happy for the young girl now that she had one. Danielle, her eyes moist with tears, turned to Jean and me, and placed her arm through mine.

"I believe we should leave them alone for a few minutes, don't you? Uncle Henri wants to speak to Maurice, I believe, and Charette needs this time too. Let's just leave them for a moment or two."

So we went through the door into the chapel, lit now with the red glow of the sanctuary lamps, and smelling of incense burning on the altar.

Sister Magdaleine came with us, and then Danielle said, "Jean, I want to take Tamar with me to help me change into Mother's bridal gown now. Will you see to Neville? He's waiting with Pierre François. You know where." She stopped, gave him a look which said much as to the precautions still being taken for his safety.

Jean smiled, pressing my hand. "Just don't ru

246

off with my love for very long, my dear Danielle," he said.

"Don't worry," she assured him. He turned and strode down the short dim hallway, and we turned into a small room near the anteroom where Henri and his children were.

The wedding gown had been pressed and laid out, still in its silk wrappings on a long wide chest, yards and yards of satin and lace, exquisitely worked in Venetian point, with tiny seed pearls embroidered on the creamy satin that glowed in the mellow candlelight that Sister Magdaleine held over it. She placed the tallow in the iron sconce and then, after exclaiming over the sheer beauty of it, the nun proceeded to help Danielle unhook her gown.

Danielle seemed like a new bride getting ready for her first nuptials; she was terribly excited as she stepped into that gown, and it fit her perfectly. She just kept smiling and I knew it was from her own inner joy at being so in love with the one man in her life.

"Oh, Tamar. Could you get me a mirror? I think I have one in my reticule, out in the anteroom. I know it is vain of me, Sister," she said to the nun, "but this gown is so special—"

"Of course, Danielle," the sister said smilingly, excitement in her brown eyes. "But I seem to recall a longer one somewhere. I shall go look for it, while Mademoiselle Tamar fetches yours, and then you shall have two." She crossed herself, and Danielle hugged her.

I dashed out into the anteroom; to my surprise, Henri and his children were not there, but I heard their voices in the chapel. It took me some minutes to discover where Danielle had left her reticule, and with it I saw the square mirror which was wrapped in a shawl. I picked them up and began walking back toward the room where she was waiting.

I heard Cameron's voice before I saw him, and I stopped in my tracks just outside the door, from where I could see Danielle's face clearly. She was pale as death. My own heart raced crazily for one maddening second, trying to recall what Cameron had said about her, but there was no time, for he was saying, ". . . I never thought to see you again, Danielle. *Mon Dieu,* but you have not changed. You are still as beautiful as I remembered you to be." His voice was low.

Her hand rested on the locket between her breasts, as if she were touching it for protection against some evil.

"André Duhamel!" she breathed in a voice that was hushed, barely audible, and had it not been for the utter stillness of the room, I might not have heard her at all. "Now I remember it all . . . It is all clear!" It was like a sudden light of revelation that came to her expression.

He was silent, and then when he spoke, his voice was rough, low. "And what do you mean by that?"

"It was you. André Duhamel. You were there, among all those . . . officers. You had been there hours before, just waiting for us, talking, telling all . . . Suzette warned us that we were in trouble. I did not see you until later, but it was you who . . .

took me. It was . . . you. . . ." Her face contorted in hatred, and she suddenly spit upon him.

His hand reached out and slapped her face in one hard resounding blow, the fingers gripping her wrists, pulling her to him. "You were that kind of woman, anyway, were you not? You gave yourself to Marc, and you would not give to me. So I took you, just as you were offering yourself to the officers. Come now. Admit it. And by God, I'll have you again before this night is out—" He broke off, and pulled her around to him with such force that I nearly fell backward in the shock of what I was witnessing.

Before I could cry out, he had pulled her through a door at the far end of the room and was dragging her away with him toward the entrance I had not seen before. She screamed then, and it shocked me into action.

I cried out, "Henri! Jean! Help— Oh, dear sweet God! Stop him—" I ran after them, but he had her firmly in his powerful grip, and even though she fought him, I could see that she was no match for him.

There were footsteps, voices, and Jean and Henri and Maurice were there, and I saw the curé out of the corner of my eye in the dim red and yellow glow of light.

"Oh, my God, he's taken her with him— Cameron and Danielle! He's mad!" I cried, throwing myself upon the door he'd gone through. But it was barred! "He's locked it—" I felt Jean's hands on me.

"He's headed for the tower!" I heard Jean say, and Henri said, "André Duhamel! Of course!"

Fear struck my heart, for I knew what he meant. "He was there that night—she remembered, after all these years, she remembered—" I couldn't go on. Henri was already running from the room. Jean said to me, his voice quiet, "Stay here, Tamar. For God's sake, stay here!" And he was off with Henri, the curé and Maurice following them and disappearing through heavy velvet curtains behind the altar.

Sister Magdaleine appeared beside me. *"Mon Dieu, mon Dieu!"* she said softly. "The viper in the nest. It was the Englishman, and not Michel, who sold us out!" She crossed herself, and ran swiftly down to the altar and threw herself down, and began to pray.

It stunned me. Where was Neville? Neville! He would have to know. My heart trembled violently. He would kill Cameron if he knew what he'd done to Danielle. I could not stay where I was; I ran down the aisle toward the altar, and went behind it.

Wall lamps like those in the sanctuary burned on the wall, and I moved through this narrow passage, knowing I was following in the wake of Jean and Henri. I walked on, trying to still my fear. Neville. Oh, Neville, my heart cried out to him, for if he lost his only love now—

I dared not let my thoughts race on in that direction.

Suddenly a figure moved out in front of me, barring my way. Shocked, I stood back. It was Nicolas.

"Mademoiselle Tamar! By God, you and I are

always meeting each other on the run, *n'est-ce pas?*" The wide grin flashed in surprise.

My heart sunk in fear, for I recalled vividly that last meeting I had with this man. He stood deliberately in my way, and I tried to move around him, but he gripped my arm tightly.

"Not so fast. Where are you running to?" The scent of wet leather and horseflesh was strong, clinging to him, and I was aware that he must have just arrived from the cliffs. But why? I had a nagging feeling that I should *know* something now, but I couldn't grasp the thought.

"I'm . . . looking for my brother. Where is he?"

Clearly he was not going to allow me to pass; he was staring at me in a very strange manner; in that greenish light, I saw the welt that my riding crop had made, and I believed he had not forgotten that I had struck him. He was wary, but I had no weapon now, so I stepped back from him.

It was then I said, "Nicolas. He—André Duhamel—has taken Danielle. It was André who betrayed the *Chouans* that night at Quiberon. For Danielle's sake, tell me where my brother is!" I began to cry.

He stared at me, aghast. "Just what are you saying?" He suddenly had both hands on my shoulders, as if he would shake the truth from me.

"Cameron—André Duhamel. He has taken Danielle with him, and Jean and the marquis have gone after him—"

"Where? *Mon Dieu!* Where?" His face was close to mine.

"To the tower—"

Nicolas suddenly let go of me and ran. I started

after him, a cold dread rippling through me as I ran blindly through that passage.

A gust of cold wet wind struck my face just as Nicolas turned back toward me, his hand on my arm, pulling me back. His voice whispered in my ear, "*Mon Dieu,* mademoiselle! Stay here! Go no further!" He pushed me against the wall, deep in the shadows.

In that split second I recognized where we were; through the opening was the dank passage from the tower chamber, and the wind gusting through it came from the open door that let in the roar of the sea and storm on those cliffs.

A single torch lit the passage, but what held both Nicolas and me back was the sudden explosion of a gun. Ahead of us I saw Henri de Rouvroy, pistol in hand. And there on the floor was the crumpled form of Cameron Pennland, next to Danielle. I saw Neville dart out of the shadows and grab his wife, and I choked a scream down inside me. I would have raced out of the room had not Nicolas's hands kept me.

It was all over; the curé rushed to Cameron and knelt over him. "He's dead."

Henri moved then. "We've no time, Jean. Hurry back to fetch Tamar. I will answer to all this. But get yourselves to the ship. Make haste. We've barely an hour to get things ready. Labbé will be called in. Hurry now. His men will come to the tower in no time, and Maurice and I and Pierre François will do our best to keep them here while you ride out in the carriage. It will be outside the old gate within a quarter of an hour."

Neville was already carrying his beloved close

to his heart, striding down the passage toward us. Jean touched his uncle's shoulder and the two men embraced, speaking to each other, but I couldn't hear what was said. Neville reached us by this time and motioned for Nicolas and me to follow.

"We must lose no time. Tamar, go to my daughter, and bring her to us in the chapel. Hurry now. Jean will help—"

Even as he spoke, Jean was at my side, and I leaned on him for support, fearing what I dreaded most, that Danielle was hurt, and I couldn't speak.

Those next hours were so unreal, and I expected to wake from it any moment. I'll never know how we managed to gather the sleeping child and her maid and smuggle them down into the old chapel, to find Sister Magdaleine working over Danielle with Nicolas and Charette standing by.

I managed to grab a heavy cloak for myself and for Danielle from somewhere. She had been revived from a dead faint with brandy and smelling salts, but she was in a state of shock as Neville picked her up and carried her into that waiting carriage.

Charette, her eyes large and luminous, clung to Jean's arm, and begged him to forgive her.

"Mademoiselle Tamar. I am . . . truly sorry. Forgive me. I . . . I told Monsieur Labbé about you and your brother. Nicolas—"

Nicolas, who was standing at her elbow, went still, and Jean looked at him. For a moment I believed there was hatred between them, but then Jean reached out to him and said, "Nicolas. You'll have to come with us, I fear. Uncle Henri has no need for . . . ex-freedom fighters now."

I touched Charette's wet cheek, and then I kissed her. "Be good to that dear papa of yours, Charette. He is a good man." And she burst into another fit of tears. My heart was full, because I knew that it had taken much for this girl to speak to me as she did.

We were just getting ready to leave the chapel, to steal furtively out of the passage, when Henri de Rouvroy rushed in.

In those next minutes we listened to Henri relate in very few words how he'd had Nicolas bring André Duhamel into the château. "I guessed he was our betrayer yesterday in the fortress. I'd given him Danielle's locket that night at Quiberon, you see. He said he'd give it to Marc. But of course he kept it, betraying us, because he'd wanted to get even with Danielle for refusing his advances.

"So we shall tell Labbé that Marc Renoire, the English agent he is waiting for, is now dead. He was shot in self-defense, and on this side of the Channel. I'm sure Neville will . . . speak of Cameron Pennland to his family with all due respect, and André Duhamel will go to the grave with Marc Renoire."

There were sudden handshakes all around, and Henri continued. "For your sakes, go speedily and know that we shall cover for you. We will say that Danielle has accompanied Jean and Tamar to Paris. Now, God go with you!"

At dawn we were aboard *L'Angélique*. I went out on the deck and Jean saw me and moved toward me. Salty wet wind sprayed my face and hair.

"You'll get drenched!" he said, laughing.

"I don't care! I love it!" I felt free and full of joy. "Where are we headed?" He came and placed his hand over mine.

"We're going to Cornwall, my love. Your brother has offered a home for this penniless ex-marquis and his bride-to-be. Will you mind so much?"

"How can I mind?" I asked. "We shall be partners in a rediscovered antique glassblowing works!" And I reminded him of the emeralds still around my neck.

"We could sell these—"

"Never! We may discover the small inheritance I am to get upon my marriage will come as a useful thing. We've lots of little subsidies, my love!" He kissed me on the mouth, holding me so tightly I never wanted him to let go.

We turned and stared out at the sea, thinking and remembering. Danielle had recovered well enough to be sleeping peacefully in the cabin, with Neville watching over her and holding his little daughter on his lap. My heart was brimming over with happiness for them and for Jean and me.

I glanced up at Jean and said, "To think that it was Cameron Pennland who somehow managed to bring that locket to Columb Manor! I'm certain he didn't think it would be discovered! I'm so very glad I found it, though!"

"And," he said as he took my face in his hands, his eyes sparkling in the early light, "I am glad too. Because it made you think of me even before I abducted you!"

"And made me your prisoner in your château!"

"You know I gave my title to my uncle, Tamar. As far as the chief of police is concerned, my uncle is still Honoré de Rouvroy, the Marquis. But the château will go to Maurice and to Charette. I am most proud of my uncle. He is a brave man."

"Of course," I agreed, and I meant it too. "He's a wonderful man."

We were silent, and I knew I wanted to ask him about Michel, so I turned and said, "Do you think it could have been Cameron after all who murdered Michel?"

It wasn't Jean who answered, but Nicolas, who had come upon us at that moment. "No, Mademoiselle Tamar. It wasn't Cameron." He said the name testily. "It . . . it was I who took Michel's life. And for my own personal reasons, to even an old score with him for selling out the Cottereau family in a misdeed which he blamed on my father. And so I paid the debt I owed Michel Cottereau."

It seemed as though he were speaking only to himself, for he stared out toward the land that was disappearing in the haze. He walked away slowly, and Jean silenced my questions with a promising kiss.